TWO LANDS

CAMBERDICE AND EARTH

LEE SHIRLEY

PARTRIDGE

A Penguin Random House Company

To order additional copies of this book, contact
Toll Free 800 101 2657 (Singapore)
Toll Free 1 800 81 7340 (Malaysia)
orders.singapore@partridgepublishing.com

www.partridgepublishing.com/singapore

For my parents and my sister

ACKNOWLEDGEMENTS

Special thanks go to my mother for supporting me through the process of publishing and to my father for sponsoring me and accompanying me both mentally and physically when I was writing in my room. Thanks to my sister for encouraging me, and thanks to all of my teachers. Thanks also to my publisher and all of my publishing consultants.

PROLOGUE

THE GROUND SHOOK and dirt rose in the cold air. She opened her eyes and looked through her window. The moon still hung high among the oak trees whose leaves swayed rhythmically. She stared at the mud-covered land. Sprouts were starting to grow, making their way through the layered dirt. She could see nothing extraordinary but a bunch of hoofmarks. Cold air leaked in through cracks around the window. She could feel it: spring was coming. It was on its way.

Horses roamed the open field. They travelled constantly, leaving nothing behind but hoofmarks. It was sad to watch them leave. She had always had a strong connection with them. People called her the horse whisperer. The horses would leave this spring and return next winter, as they did every year. Each time they returned, there were a few members added to the herd.

The legend said that horses left the land but always returned. If they did not, then things were bad.

THE LEGEND OF TWO LANDS

Once upon a time, Carisie, the goddess of the wind, invited horses to settle in Camberdice, a magical place where innocents lived. The place was linked to a portal that allowed creatures to travel from Camberdice to Earth. Humans were close allies with equines, who brought peace and hope to Earth and turned what had once been darkness into happiness. A century passed with equines travelling from one end of the portal to the other to visit their human companions.

One day, the Son of Earth was born. He was meant to lead the people and guard them with his name and his power. But he was born on the eclipse. The darkness that blocked out the sun caused him to be evil; the eclipse gave him dark power with which to rule the world.

That same year, Carisie's daughter was born. She was born with the sun, casting a glow around her. She was meant to connect the people, to defeat the dark with intelligence. But at the age of five, she became lost; she disappeared and left no trace behind. Carisie's husband died and Carisie and her people lost hope. They believed that Carisie's daughter, Carisa, had been hauled into Earth. They sealed the portal; they would rather be isolated than be in darkness.

AUGUST

AUGUST HAD SURVIVED on her own for years before being adopted. Her parents had found her on the street somewhere and taken her in. They had wanted a child of their own, so they adopted her and named her August, after the month when they had found her. They didn't know her her real name or her exact age.

"When I found you, you were a strong girl. Your blonde hair glowed like the sun. It almost seemed like you were protected. We believed that God had led us to you. You were a gift to us," her mom told her. "You used to repeat the same word again and again. *Camberdice*—I think that's what you said."

August's parents, Janette and Jake, were brunette and blond respectively. They estimated that August was five when they adopted her. It was just the three of them in the family. They also had a hound named Dark and a little cat named Bobby.

"You've always had a strong connection with horses," her mother said once, when she was eight years old. "I wonder why?

When you first arrived, you saw a wild horse near our backyard. Instead of running away, you reached out to it. Then whenever that stallion saw you, he ran towards you. You were able to tame him at such a young age!"

August's hair was a bright goldish blonde. Her skin was a light peach, almost white, and her lips were pinkish red. Her eyes were dark purple, which was very unusual. People at school called her a wild child because of her eyes. Others even called her a freak. She hated school; she was not welcomed by anyone. August's mom would sit beside the bed, listen to August's worries, and hum songs she made up to soothe her. August's father always made sure when he picked her up that that she didn't have bruises and hadn't been bullied. They loved August and tried to protect her.

A Morning Surprise

AUGUST'S EYES OPENED to face the spinning fan. She dragged herself lazily across the room and into the bathroom. It was a splendid Saturday morning. The winter was ending and soon flowers would be blooming and birds would be chirping happily. She opened her closet, picked out a denim jacket, a T-shirt, and a pair of jeans, and got dressed. As she raced down the stairs towards the living room, she passed a row of paintings on the wall.

August's mom, Janette, was preparing pancakes in the kitchen. Her dad was reading his newspaper and, as usual, not paying much attention to his surroundings.

"Oh, you're awake. Care for some pancakes before you head out?" Janette greeted August with a kiss on the forehead and handed her a plate of pancakes. "Blueberry jam?"

"Yes, please. Hey, I had a really weird dream yesterday." August sat down at the table.

Janette placed the jar of jam on the table and handed August a fork. She smiled and eyed August's tangled hair. "As usual, my

daughter does not care to brush her hair at all. Go ahead." She
began combing August's hair with her fingers.

"There was this book, an old book bound in leather," August
said. "I opened it and then a strong force was pulling me inside it.
I entered a totally different world! There were horses everywhere.
The people there had dark-blue eyes, except for a lady in a
white-and-gold gown with bright-blue eyes who walked towards
me. With her was a man with dark-purple eyes just like mine.
And then I woke up." She dug her fork into the pancakes.

"That's a weird one. Just like the legend about the place
where the horses live. The woman sounds like the goddess
Carisie."

"You mean the goddess of the wind?" August stopped
chewing and turned her head. Her mother had read the Legend
of Camberdice to her ever since she was a young child.

"I think it's time to tell you the truth."

Janette rose from her seat and walked into her study. August
followed close behind. Janette reached for the tallest shelf of the
bookcase and pulled something down. She handed it to August.
It was small enough to fit in her palm and had a lock on its front
side.

"There you go," Janette said. "And here is the key." She
reached down her shirt collar and pulled out a chain. There,
dangling at the end of the chain, was a tiny key. She removed it,
placed it in August's hand, and smiled. "Go ahead."

August inserted the key into the box's keyhole and turned it
clockwise. The metal tab of the lock flipped open. The box lid
began to open even though August hadn't touched it.

"Whoa, did you see that? It lifted all on its own!" Inside the
box lay a necklace. It was a glowing purple stone on a gold chain,

and the name "Carisa" was carved on it. August looked at her mother apprehensively, her hands trembling.

"Look on the back," Janette commanded.

August carefully turned over the purple stone. It glowed brightly in her palm. On it was carved the word "Camberdice."

August gasped and covered her mouth with her hand.

"Am I . . . the lost child?"

WHO AM I?

"I DON'T KNOW, MY child. You were wearing this when we found you and took you home. The answer to that question is for you to discover," Janette said, tears filling her eyes.

"So the legend is true. I can't believe it!"

"Darling, we're not sure about that yet. Your purple eyes, your connection with horses—I thought at first they were just coincidences. But maybe, just maybe . . ."

"I am really the goddess's lost child."

Janette leaned forward and gave her daughter a tight hug. "C'mon, put it on." She took the necklace and fastened it around August's neck. "Beautiful, as always."

Camberdice . . . the word August had mumbled as a child. She didn't have much memory about her childhood. If she really were the lost child, then it seemed that having been on Earth surrounded by humans had brainwashed her. She wanted to know who she truly was. Deep down, though, she felt that it must be true, that the purple of her eyes explained who she had been all along and where she really belonged. *Am I just crazy, or is it the truth? Am I truly the goddess's lost child, or am I just hoping for the impossible? I was taught to believe in the legend, but what if it's not real? And if I really am Carisa, will I be expelled from society? Will people believe that I am a wild child and burn me at the stake? If I tell people that I am the bridge that will connect two worlds, won't they think I'm insane and call me a freak?*

August put the necklace under her shirt as if protecting it from the cold. She was still in shock, but she appreciated how her mother had confessed the truth to her. She had always wanted to be normal, to be just like other children. Yet now, she felt excited to learn that she probably was somebody different and special—although the thought made her scared and worried too. But for the moment, she decided to try to get on with her day.

"I have to walk Dark and Bobby. I guess we'll figure this out later." She really needed some fresh air to help her think and function better.

"The legend says that Carisa will return," Janette said. "If you truly are her, then there's no way to escape the words. The portal will find you eventually. There's no point worrying about it."

As they walked back to the kitchen, August thought about all the times she had been bullied for looking different. One tall, beautiful girl at school had used to tease her intensely, saying, "What on earth are you? So ugly!" *Now I know the answer,* she thought. *I might be a creature from Camberdice.*

She sat back down at the kitchen table. Her mother had purchased it long ago from a thrift shop near the house. It was made of oak and had beautiful angels carved into its surface. One corner of the tabletop was missing; August's dear dog, Dark, had decided to chew it off. But the table was still a masterpiece. It had been carved by an Italian named Vangresont. August and her parents found the name funny and always made fun of it, pronouncing it *Van-greee-sont*.

The pancakes were now cold and the blueberry jam had hardened. "Warm it? Or cold-eat?" Janette asked. That was her way of asking, "Do you want to warm it or do you want to eat it cold?"

"Warm it and warm-eat," August replied, meaning, "I want them warm." She handed her mom the plate.

The family pets were already waiting for August to take them outside. Dark wagged his tail, and Bobby jumped onto the table. August always said the cat was a ninja; anybody who ever played with him understood what she meant. He would jump high up onto tables and chairs. He could be sitting right in front of you and vanish the very next second. Ninja skills were in his blood.

August put her elbow on the table and leaned her chin on her hand. She looked out the fogged window and watched the kids playing football in the field. She had always wanted to play football, but nobody ever wanted to play with her, not even during PE.

August's dad, Jake, came over and dropped a stack of letters on the kitchen table.

"The top one's yours," he said to August. "Want to exercise in the park with me?" He lifted Bobby off the table and placed him gently onto the floor. "Go play with Dark. Go!"

August nodded and grabbed the topmost letter on the stack. "To my dearest August Larson" was typed neatly onto the envelope. She tore off the glued tab and pulled out the letter.

Dear Grandchild,

Heyo, my love! Sending love from Texas. How are you doing? Grand-dada and Grand-mama miss you terribly. I miss your laughter and your amazing smile. You are turning thirteen soon—an early happy birthday to you, my love! How's your life going? Planning to date soon? Let me tell you something: never *ever* date a guy like your Grand-dada. I'm just kidding. I stil love him. Remember the time we baked together? You were only six. Grand-dada and I are going to Hawaii soon as an anniversary mini 'moon. We just want you to know that we'll always, always, always love you, no matter what! You're my dearest child and always will be.

Oh, I just learned a new word. The kids around my neighborhood tell me that "BTW" means by the way. I learned some other ones, too, like "OMG," "WTH," and "srsly." Never too old to learn new stuff! Hope to hear from you soon. Have a great thirteenth birthday. We'll visit you soon—please do prepare my favourite cake, red velvet with cream cheese.

All right, now your Grand-dada wants me to pass the letter to him. I'll stop writing now. See you in a bit!

Grand-dada: Don't listen to your Grand-mama. I'm a nice guy. You know that.

Lots of love from Texas,
Your Grand-dada and Grand-mama

August read the letter and placed it back in the envelope. "A letter from Grand-mama and Grand-dada," she said as she handed it to Jake, who was sipping from a freshly brewed cup of coffee.

"What did they say?"

"Just something like a greeting."

Jake nodded and began to read the letter. August settled back in her chair to wait for her mother to finish re-heating the pancakes.

After breakfast, she grabbed the pets' collars from the hook and secured them around each pet's neck. Then she buckled the long leashes in place.

"Dad, we're good to go," she announced. Jake hurried over to put on his boots, and then they were off.

Outside, the snow was melting, robins chirped happily above the trees, and the pets were happy to be returning to their playground. It had been months since August had let them out for a walk. It was too hard to walk when the snow was piled high. But now, the weather was grand. She inhaled deeply and packed her lungs with the morning breeze. Everything smelled right. Spring was on its way. Flower buds were beginning to poke their way through the snow.

Still, worries were circling August's brain as she walked beside her father on the pavement. It was quiet except for the sound of trees brushing against each other.

"What's wrong today?" Jake asked.

"Nothing's wrong. I just don't feel like talking right now."

The rest of the walk went well. Flowers were blooming. The wind blew softly against their cheeks. After thirty minutes, they returned home.

For the rest of the day, August thought about who she truly was. Was she Carisa? She tried to figure out a way to find out whether this was true, but nothing came to mind.

She tried to shake off her anxieties as she went to bed holding the necklace tight in her hands. It was glowing, creating a tunnel of light in the darkness.

"Wait a minute . . ." August jumped out of bed and sprinted downstairs. She raced to her mother's study and pulled out *The Legend of Two Lands*. A legend that her mother adored, she would always read it to August when she was younger. "The spell—the one that opens and closes the portal! If I am truly Carisa, I will be able to open it."

Her happy chirping to herself attracted her mother.

"August Junior, what do you think you're doing creeping into my study at this hour?" August's happy chirping had awoken her mother, who now entered the room in a silk robe with her hair in curlers.

August knew she was in trouble when her mom used her full name. "I'm not doing anything bad, Mom—chill. I'm just curious about the spell. The spell in the legend that opens and closes the portal."

"Oh, you want to see if you can open the portal. I see. Go ahead, then: page 493."

"Wait, how do you know the page number of the spell?" August and her mother and had always been close. They were best friends and they always would be.

"I've told you a thousand times: I read them all the time."

"Yes, ma'am." August nodded and opened the book to page 493. She and her mother read silently.

The Spell of Two Lands' Souls

A book lays its way
In the dark and in the day.
Purple guides, dark blue's the trail,
But for one who controls, she isn't frail.

One who guides the sun and wind,
Not delicate, but strong—
In a place where Carisie belongs,
She lays the way, places the path where she'll win.

The child of the land
Slipped away from Carisie's hand.
She'll find her way;
She'll be on her way.

Was August the "she" in the spell? She wasn't sure. But if she were destined to find the way, the portal to Camberdice, then she was also destined to fight the Son of Earth. She and her mom looked at each other at the same time.

"'A book lays its way'. So the portal to Camberdice might be hidden somewhere in a book," August said.

"'She'll find her way; She'll be on her way'. I guess that's for you, my dear," Janette said. "This spell is definitely talking about you."

"If the spell was written according to my story . . ."

"You'll be the one to find it. And the way is in a book."

"So I am the 'child of the land'?"

"The land of Camberdice."

"Shall I give it a shot?"

Janette hestitated, looking away from August.

"What is it?" August questioned.

"I don't want to lose my child," Janette replied. Tears started to roll down her cheeks.

"You won't, Mom."

"You'll probably find your biological mother and father. Just don't forget about us. We'll always be on the other side. Just remember that."

"Oh, Mom, I will never, ever forget about you or Dad. You will still always be my parents," August reassured.

"Go ahead and try to open the portal," Janette said.

August read the spell out loud, pronouncing each syllable clearly. After she finished, she waited a few seconds for something big to happen. She could feel her heart beating against her chest. Her feet were cold and numb. But the room was still; nothing moved. Even the oak trees outside the window remained quiet.

"Nothing happened!" Janette exclaimed.

An owl hooted from the tree outside. It observed them through the window carefully with its head cocked. Its eyes shone brightly in the dark as if it were warning them. It creeped August out. She shivered and reached up to her neck to feel the warmth of the necklace. Suddenly a light bulb went off in her head.

"Wait a minute. 'Purple guides, dark blue's the trail'!" Her heart skipped a beat. The wise owl spread its wings and flew away.

"What does that mean?"

"Purple's the necklace! The stone is purple. Dark blue is the book because its cover is dark blue!"

"You're so smart!"

"You've had a smart daughter all along and it's just now that you're discovering it?" August stuck her tongue out at Janette.

"OK, here we go." She held the stone in her hand and read the spell over again, this time from memory. As she recited, she could feel the stone grow warmer. It began to cast a bright purple light. The old leatherbound book vibrated.

"'She'll find her way; She'll be on her way.'" By the time she finished the last two sentences, she was wrapped in a purple glow. The blue of the book merged in and swallowed her whole. She felt pain building up in her body. Her skin began to tear.

"It's the Breakdown! You will be there in no time!" Janette yelled. She was watching from across the room with her hands clutched over her chest.

"*Mom!*" That was the last word August managed to say before she passed out from the excruciating pain attacking her entire body.

An Open Field

AUGUST'S SHATTERED BODY fragments lay in the grass. The Breakdown wasn't complete yet. The last stage was about to happen. The fragments glowed purple and merged together to form a silhouette and then, in a split second, a completely motionless body. August had entered Camberdice. She found herself lying on the grass, her hand still holding the necklace. She could feel a horse galloping nearby; the ground shook as the horse's hooves pounded on the dirt. August didn't have the strength to get up.

The horse was coming closer to her lifeless body. It slowed into a trot and then halted directly over her. It nickered at August, then lowered its head to touch August's arm with its muzzle, and nickered again. She tried but could give no reply. The stallion lowered its head again and gently pushed August. She still could not move. The stallion let out a loud neigh, then galloped around the field. It reared on its hind legs and bolted.

August heard a boy's voice calming the horse down in the distance. The sounds of the boy and the horse became louder until suddenly the boy was standing over her. His eyes were blue and he was gaping at her. She found that she finally had the strength to speak again.

"Well, this is kind of awkward. My name's August."

"It's nice to meet you. I'm Matt. Your eyes—they're different."

August liked the sound of his voice and she smiled a little. She could feel her cheeks flush.

"They are. Even in here."

"What's that you're wearing?"

"You mean this?" August lifted the purple pendant and showed it to Matt. His face turned pale.

"Oh, My Goddess, this can't be true!"

"Calm down, bro, it's just a necklace."

"No, it's not. You're the lost child!"

"Oh. I guess now I finally have the answer to my question."

"Your eyes explain it all. Can't you see? You're Carisa!"

"I know, I probably am. But I've only just arrived. Can you at least bring me to a hotel or something?"

"What?"

"A *hotel?*"

"What's that?"

"Never mind." She shrugged. "Can you bring me to some shelter where I'll be safe?"

"No shelter—we're going to Candrale!" Matt exclaimed. Without explaining, he grabbed August's arm and started running, leading her to Candrale.

THE REUNION

CARISIE, THE GODDESS of the wind, was sitting on her throne when a guard rushed into the room and stared at her with eyes that were filled with tears and shock. He nodded to her. The goddess instantly stood up, picked up her skirts, and rushed towards the closed door.

"My Goddess, do you need your mount?" the guard asked, hurrying after her.

"No thank you, there's no need of it. I can walk." She went down the stairs and out the palace door. "Where is she?" she asked the guard.

"At the gate, My Goddess."

Carisie kicked off her shoes and ran as fast as she could until she reached the steel gate. She caught a glimpse of a girl and boy and stopped for a moment. "Oh my." Then she began walking again, faster and faster, until she reached them. Carisie knelt down and hugged the girl tight. She felt something strong and bold connecting their souls together, so she knew for sure that this girl was her daughter.

"I will never lose you again, never," Carisie said. Her daughter hugged her back, trembling. "I will never allow anybody to harm you again." Carisie kissed her daughter's forehead. "Beautiful Carisa, you're back! Your eyes are just like mine. You were the only child in Camberdice with purple eyes. You truly are my long-lost child." She placed her delicate fingers on her child's cheek. "How I wish Paul could be here to see you," she murmured.

WHO'S PAUL?

P AUL. THE NAME echoed in August's brain. *Is he my father?*
My grandfather? She knew that she belonged in Camberdice
and that her biological mother was Carisie. Part of her wanted
to return to Earth, which she called home, but she was bound
to this place and had a responsibility to protect it. She couldn't
leave her real mother again. It would be too much for Carisie to
handle.

Matt stood rooted to the ground. He bowed to the goddess
and greeted the guard.

"So you're the one who brought Carisa here, young boy?" The
goddess's voice was as soft and tender as harp strings being plucked.

"Yes, My Lady," Matt replied. He looked at his new friend
and grinned.

"Thank you so much! A reward is owed. Tell me, what do
you want?"

Matt shrugged. "I have only one request. May I be your
daughter's friend?" he asked politely.

August was surprised. Her mother agreed and told Matt he was now Carisa's new friend.

"*August,* my name is August. That's what I want to be called."

Carisie looked into August's eyes and sighed sorrowfully. "All right, my dear. August, I will give you a tour around the palace and a brief history of Camberdice. Would you like to come along, boy?" Matt accepted the offer and joined August's side.

Although the reunion had been emotional, August did not cry. She believed that crying was equivalent to failure and that tears showed weakness. She would never again cry for a missing mother. Now that August had found her real mother, she wondered if Carisie would be anything like her mom back on Earth. Would she give August a warm breakfast and a morning kiss? Would she be August's personal counsellor? August didn't like having to leave her parents behind, but she didn't want to let Carisie down, and she wanted the best for Earth.

August wasn't sure if she would like Camberdice, but she couldn't escape what had been written in *The Legend of Two Lands.* She had to stay in order to bring peace, not only to this land, but also to Earth. She was destined to fight the Son of Earth. It was all a matter of time. How soon would she be facing the battle? She cleared her thoughts and carried on along the path.

THE LEGEND OF CARISIE,
GODDESS OF THE WIND

ONCE UPON A time, a child was born with the wind. The wind cast her body, giving her the power to bring peace. She was called Carisie. She had bright, blonde hair and light-blue eyes, and she was known to be wise and just. She was raised by an ordinary woman in Camberdice, but on her eighteenth birthday, she gained her power. Her life turned upside down; she would never be the same again. She was crowned the goddess of the wind. She would be the bright light that guided her people.

Graceful and wise, she was known as the noble goddess. She rode unicorns and glided through the wind. She brought peace to Camberdice by releasing white doves. At a young age, she was married to Paul, the god of the sun. She protected her land with her life and invited horses to live there. Then she brought them to Earth to acompany the lonely humans.

She was one of the Rulers, a trio of goddesses who led Camberdice together. The other two were Meraida, goddess of the water, and Oakastine, goddess of the woods. The three were close friends. Together, they protected the magical land with their names and their power, trying to defeat the darkness.

THE PALACE

T HEY WALKED IN single file, the goddess leading the way
back to the palace. August looked all around her. There was
a marble fountain surrounded by a stone path. On top of the
fountain was an angel stepping on clouds. August peered at it
more closely. The angel was holding a child wrapped in a scarf.
The scarf was incredibly detailed; flowers and patterns were
carefully carved into the stone.

"This fountain was built to remember you, Caris—August,"
Carisie announced.

August leaned forward and placed her palm into the clear
water of the fountain. "Thanks for calling me August. I really
appreciate that." She cleared her throat. It felt stuck. She couldn't
find the right words to communicate what she wanted to say.
It was as if she had lost her voice. She wasn't sure if what she
said would be appropriate or not. She wanted to be polite in
this foreign place. Before she knew the customs of Camberdice,
perhaps it would be better to keep quiet.

"Take this stone," Carisie said. She handed August a pebble and gestured her forward. "Make a wish and throw it into the fountain. Maybe your wish will come true."

August took a step back and turned around, holding the pebble tightly in her palm. She could feel its texture: smooth, slippery, cold, and with a sharp edge. *I wish to see my parents again,* she thought. *I want to win the battle I will be facing.* She threw the pebble over her left shoulder and heard it hit the water's surface with a plop.

Things were different here in Camberdice. Instead of throwing coins into a fountain, they used pebbles. There were no hotels here, either. Matt hadn't understood that word. A thousand thoughts raced through her mind. *Do they have pizza? Do they understand the word "computer"? Do they know about Facebook?* Without Facebook, life would be extremely boring. Without a computer, how would she play music? She couldn't imagine life without music. And the thought that she might never again have a bite of pizza, her favourite food, haunted her brain. She imagined eating a piece of pizza, gulping down the mozzarella. *Mmm . . .* The idea that she wouldn't ever do it again broke her heart.

"August?" Carisie waved her fingers in front of August's eyes.

"Yes, I'm here. Sorry, I was just thinking about something." She put her hands in her pyjamas' pocket.

"Do you make wishes like this at . . . home?" Carisie asked, her light-blue eyes gazing into August's.

August could tell that Carisie was trying to make her comfortable. She tried to find words they would understand.

"Yes, we do. But instead of throwing a pebble, we throw a coin."

"Oh, that's interesting! Maybe you can teach us more about your lifestyle back on Earth. Well, let's move on."

The stone path back to the palace stretched for miles. On either side there were aspen trees with their pink and orange leaves trimmed into cone shapes. Camberdice had never experienced winter. It was a land stuck in spring and summer. The goddess of the wind controlled the amount of wind that blew, the goddess of water controlled the amount of rainfall, and the goddess of the woods controlled the growth of crops.

As they walked, white parakeets flew above them. To their right was a white stag grazing. Its thin, tall antlers curved beautifully and on its forehead was a gold marking: a picture of roses bunched together to form a diamond shape. August gasped in amazement.

"This is my mount," said Carisie. "Her name is Gloria. You'll soon receive a mount, August. It will be a stag just like mine."

Everything seemed so white. Matt was wearing white, Carisie was wearing white with gold, and her stag was white. August was the only exception; she wasn't wearing any white but was in her pyjamas and bed slippers.

They walked for what seemed like hours until finally they reached the glowing-white palace. The guards in front opened the doors. They were grand, approximately forty feet tall and twenty-five feet wide, made of brown wood carved with roses, and had handles of pure diamond.

Inside, marble tiles shone with gloss. A statue of a goddess mounting a stag stood at the entrance, and behind it was a flight of marble stairs. August looked up at the high ceiling. It was painted with unicorns, stags, pegasuses, and cherubs. August observed each breathtaking decoration carefully. She had never in her life visited a place as grand as Candrale. She gasped as she caught a glimpse of a painting. The subject was a purple-eyed baby girl in a golden glow surrounded by white roses. *Is that me?* She did not dare to ask.

Carisie led the way up the flight of stairs and through a hall of paintings. She stopped in front of a door and smiled at August. "This will be your room." She turned the golden doorknob and invited them in.

"You're lucky, Carisa. I don't even have my own room at home," Matt said, shoving his hands into his pockets.

"August, my name is August."

"Sorry, August."

"It's OK. We all make mistakes."

"Young boy, may I know your name?" the goddess asked politely.

"Sorry, My Lady, my name is Matt."

"Matt, it's time for you to return home. It's getting dark now; the moon will soon appear. Your mother will be worried. Guards, please send this young boy home. I want him to be safe. But feel free to visit again, Matt."

And Matt was led away by the guards.

PAUL

AUGUST WAVED GOODBYE to Matt and then turned her attention to Carisie. Her real mother was wearing a white gown that was embroidered with gold and had a train. Her blonde hair fell perfectly over her shoulders; it was long, wavy, and shiny. Her crown shone brightly with purple, blue, and white gems and crystals. Her smile was bright and warm, and her eyes were a beautiful shade of blue.

Carisie invited August into the room and sat down on a cushioned chair while August looked around. The bed was a four-poster with curtains tied up at each corner. Above the bed hung a painting of a white stag, and underneath the painting was a shiny gold plate. August touched the ivy-patterned white-linen bedspread. Beside the bed was a white-and-gold table holding a lamp with a lace lampshade. In the corner of the room was a white dresser painted with gold designs.

"Well, August, I think it's time to tell you about your father," Carisie said softly. She was holding a box in her hands. August sat down on the bed to face her. "Your father, Paul, was a great warrior. He was also known as the god of the sun. He protected Camberdice from the darkness. He protected both Camberdice and Earth from the Son of Earth, an evil human being with dark power, by casting a layer of glow onto Earth and Camberdice each day. In this way, the darkness was kept away, although it couldn't be controlled." Carisie paused and looked at the box.

"One day, the darkness reached a climax: the eclipse. Paul knew that sacrifices were necessary to keep others from dying, so he used all of his might to cast the brightest glow he had ever created. The glow spread through Camberdice and Earth and reversed the eclipse. The sun appeared again, but your father . . . disappeared." With tears in her eyes, she opened the box. "In this book he wrote down the spell to cast glow. I preserved his book for you, knowing you would return one day." She placed the box on August's lap and held her hand.

"Is the glow still there?" August asked. "My father's glow, I mean. Is it still there?"

"Yes, but it won't last forever. You were born with the sun, so you are the only person now who can cast glow. You will be our saviour."

"How?" August croaked, trembling.

"You must learn how. The battle between you and the Son of Earth won't be easy. I'll guide you and teach you to hunt. I will never again watch you slip out of my hands." She placed her warm fingers on August's cheek. "Never."

"When will my training start?"

"Whenever I think you are ready."

"What must I know in order to be ready?"

"First you'll need to learn everything about Camberdice. It's far different from Earth. You'll need to be familiar with your surroundings. Don't worry, I will teach you." Carisie patted August's hand. "Come now, I'll show you something."

THE HEARTBREAKING POEM

AUGUST ROSE FROM her bed and followed her mother down the hallway. At the end of the hall stood a tall door guarded by two stag statues. The doorknob was golden, and a bright golden plate was mounted on the door. The stags were beautifully carved and very realistic. They looked more like taxidermy than statues. Their antlers were strong and bold, their eyes lively. Carisie opened the grand door and then stepped aside.

"The door's opened for the Lady," announced Carisie. She gestured her daughter into the room and followed her in. Then she shut the door behind them. August noticed something hanging on the wall; her curiosity pushed her forward to examine it. It was a printed poem sealed in a golden frame. She read it aloud.

Loss, Sorrow, and Tears

The sunlight gathered,
Both of my loves entered,
Entered my life and my heart.
I never knew that one day both of you would part.

One man whom I loved,
One child whom I lost,
One land which I guide;
One hundred words to describe.

My life has fallen into misery,
My emotions crumbled like pastries;
My husband dead and never found,
My child lost in a foreign land, never found.

No one could understand my sorrow.
I have to stay strong to guide my fellows;
Tears have dried out,
Hopes have run out.

I'll stay bold and strong
To guard this land where I belong.

August finished the poem, and Carisie, who had sat back and closed her eyes, opened them.

"Well read, very well read indeed," Carisie complimented. She rose from her seat.

"What's it about?"

"You and your father."

"Oh. I'm sorry to ask."

"No, no, it's OK. I got over it. I still miss him, but you can't fool death. You can't revive the dead."

"How did you meet him?"

"It's a long story."

"Do you mind telling it to me?"

"No, not at all." Carisie took a deep breath and began. "Your father and I met on a beach. He was sitting alone on a rock, looking out to sea. His purple eyes caught my attention, so I began to talk to him. When he smiled at me, his smile was so handsome that it took my breath away. I knew he liked me too because he couldn't stop staring at me. We sat on the rock together for the entire evening and watched the sunset. As soon as we met, I really liked him. And . . ."

"And?"

"That's how we met."

"That's sweet."

"I'm glad you liked the story."

THE DOVE LETTER

THE GODDESS LAID a piece of paper on the table, as well as a dark-purple quill and a bottle of ink. She then sat down and began to write.

"August, I'm writing a dove letter," she said.

"What's a dove letter?" asked August.

"It's a letter that will be sent by a dove. I'm inviting Matt to ride with us tomorrow. We'll be taking a ride to explore the village. He can keep you company."

August nodded and began to watch Carisie carefully, obeserving each move she made.

In a few seconds, the letter was done. "There!" Carisie handed the letter to August.

An Invitation for a Ride:

Dear Matt, I can't thank you enough for bringing my daughter back. As an extra reward, I am inviting you for a ride to the village. Please come along. The ride will be tomorrow evening at three tims. We will prepare a mount for you. The guards will lead you to us.

Best wishes from Carisie, the goddess of the wind

"What's a *tim?*" August asked curiously.

"That's how we measure time. Now, roll up the letter and tie a ribbon around it," Carisie ordered, handing a piece of gold ribbon to August. "I'll teach you how to send it."

August rolled the paper carefully into a cylinder, wrapped the gold ribbon around the cylinder, and tied the ribbon into a bow. She returned the letter to Carisie.

"Well done." Carisie patted August's shoulder. "We'll release it now. Let's go."

August followed Carisie out of the room. She liked her real mother, she really did. She was starting to trust Carisie and maybe, just maybe, to feel that she loved her. They passed through hall after hall and finally reached the winding staircase.

"Do you want to play a game?" Carisie asked playfully.

"Sure." August wondered what the game would be.

"Then just stand still and enjoy." Carisie murmured under her breath. A cloud appeared beneath August and travelled down the staricase, carrying August with it. Carisie, too, made a cloud for herself. She raced down the stairs and reached the bottom before August.

"That was awesome!" exclaimed August. The clouds disappeared.

"I'm glad that you liked it." Carisie laughed, and August grinned from ear to ear.

"How did you do that?" August was desperate to know.

"It was a spell. I can do lots of things with wind and clouds. I was born with the power," Carisie answered with a grin.

"Wow! Can I do that too?"

"I don't know, my child. You were born with the sun, so your powers might be related to light. You're still very young. You'll have to learn the basics, such as casting glow. Then you can play with your powers and try to discover something new. You'll learn to cast glow soon. We'll figure out what your father wrote in that book and start from there."

"OK," August said without thinking twice. She wasn't afraid to speak anymore; she had found her voice and her courage.

"Let's go now before the sun sets."

August took her mother's hand. Carisie turned her head in surprise. "That feels good, you holding my hand. I had forgotten the feeling of it, but now I remember." Carisie folded her fingers against August's; ten fingers were clasped together. The twosome then went out the door together.

THE DOVE BELL

Outside, August and her mother walked side by side, holding hands. They passed through the row of trees and entered a paddock where white stags were grazing. One stag galloped around the paddock; another reared up on its hind legs. They trotted elegantly, lifting their feet high; they almost seemed to be floating. Then they slowed down and began to walk gracefuly. In the middle of the field stood a tall steel pole. Hanging from the pole was a golden bell.

Carisie led August in and closed the fence behind them. The stags stopped what they were doing to look at August with curiosity. When they saw Carisie, they bowed and began to graze again. August followed her mother to the pole and handed her the rolled letter.

"To call for the letter doves, you ring this gold bell. The clear and loud *ting* alerts the doves and they find their way to the bell. You just have to give them a couple of minutes to arrive."

THE LEGEND OF THE
LETTER BIRDS

I N THE QUIET and peaceful land of Camberdice, letter doves settled down high up in the oak trees. They had paper-white feathers, dark-green eyes, and light-pink curved beaks. They rose with the morning sun and roosted when the moon climbed the sky. They worked at dawn and rested when the moon rose. They played an important role in Camberdice: they helped people to send letters to their desired destinations. They flew with great speed across the blue sky, faster than hawks, faster than eagles.

THE LETTER DOVE

CARISIE PULLED THE golden bell's handle and it rang loud, clear, and harmonious. The ring echoed and she stepped back, laying her palm on August's back.

"Just wait, they will come."

August stared at the wide orange sky. The sun was about to set. Far off, a silhouette began to form. It was a bird flying rapidly, travelling through clouds, racing with the wind. The bird folded its wings and dove towards the steel pole. Then the fearless bird opened its wings for a light and steady landing; with a *tap*, the bird landed on its claws. Its wings were white as snow, its claws strong as metal, its eyes green as the forest. *What a beautiful creature*, August thought, astonished. She carefully touched the bird's feathers. They were soft as cotton, smooth as silk. She had never seen a dove like this before. It was breathtaking.

Carisie stretched her arm towards the majestic bird and allowed it to step onto her hand. "Watch closely," she warned as she lifted the bird. She whispered into the bird's ear. "Please send this letter to Matt. Thank you."

August watched as the dove lifted off her mother's fingers and flew upwards into the orange sky. It slowly disappeared from her sight.

"And that's your first lesson. Next time you'll be the one who writes and sends." Carisie's eyes gleamed, reflecting the setting sun. "Tomorrow we'll learn more. Let's go home now. You can take a shower and then we'll have dinner."

Carisie opened her hand, and August held it tightly. Then mother and child exited the paddock and headed for the palace.

A CREAM-COLOURED DRESS

Dusk approached, stretching out August and Carisie's dark shadows to be miles long as they walked. The trees were silent, and the birds were nowhere to be seen.

Back at the palace, August was led to her room. She had a warm and comforting shower. The water smelled like lavender. When she stepped out of the shower, she found a dress lying across her bed. Her mother must had asked a maid to bring it to her.

"Now I don't have to walk around in pyjamas," August said. She picked up the satin dress. It was as soft and smooth as the letter dove's feathers had been, and it, too, had the light and soothing scent of lavender. The dress was cream-coloured and sleeveless with a V-shaped collar surrounded by ruffles. She slipped into the divine dress and looked at her reflection in the mirror. The bottom of the dress reached her toes. She turned to look at the short train in the back of the dress.

As she admired her own reflection, there was a knock at the door.

"Yes?"

A soft voice said, "I am here to take you to the dining room."

"I'm coming." August hurried over to open the door. A petite girl with blue eyes, perky lips, and brown hair stood before her. She had her hair tied up into a neat bun, and she was wearing a plain white dress and white shoes.

"The goddess also sent you these shoes." She passed August a pair of cream-coloured flats. August put them on and then followed the girl down the hall.

"What's your name?" August asked. She smiled at the petite girl.

"Traise, that's my name," the girl replied with a slanty grin. They went down a hall full of portraits and turned left at the next corner.

"What a beautiful name!"

"Thanks. Would you like me to call you Lady Carisa or Lady August?"

"August, please."

"Yes, My Lady."

"Quit it with the 'Lady.' 'August' will do."

"You're so humble . . . August."

"I'm just not used to having a title."

They walked through a corridor filled with statues and turned right.

"The dining room is just up there," Traise said, pointing a boney finger towards a set of tall wooden doors. On either side of the doors stood two statues of pegasuses with outspread wings rearing on their hind feet. Traise knocked on the doors three times—*knock, knock, knock*—and opened them.

In the dining room, Carisie rose from her seat. "August, you're here just in time." She clasped her hands together and welcomed

August. "Thank you, Traise. Would you like to have dinner with us?"

"But it's not appropriate for me to share the same table as you, My Goddess. I'm a maid."

"Don't be silly! You are always welcome. Come on, I don't bite. Neither does August," Carisie said.

"Thank you, I appreciate it," Traise said.

"Come on in, then." Carisie offered Traise her hand and led her to the table. *Carisie is so kind!* August had never met anybody as kind as Carisie. She admired Carisie's beauty and elegance, her wisdom, and her compassion for the people of her land.

THE PLATE OF GREENS

AUGUST SAT DOWN in a red armchair facing Carisie. Traise sat beside August, keeping her head lowered and avoiding eye contact. Above the dining table hung an enormous chandelier made of thousands of pure diamonds which sparkled brilliantly in the bright white light.

Several chefs entered the room carrying trays of food and beverages. They placed the covered dishes on the dining table and disappeared again before August was able to thank them. The smell of warm vegetables lifted into the air.

"This looks grand. Shall we start?" Carisie said.

"Hold your horses, aren't we supposed to pray before we eat?" August protested. Her parents, Janette and Jake, were strict Catholics. She had been raised to thank God for the food before she ate.

"Why?"

"At home, we always pray before we have a meal."

"All right, let's do it," Carisie said. "Then I can learn something new too."

August joined hands with Carisie and Traise and told them to do the same. "Carisie, give Traise your other hand. Lord, we thank you for the gifts of your bounty, which we enjoy at this table. As you have provided for us in the past, so may you sustain us throughout our lives. While we enjoy your gifts, let us not forget the needy and those in want. Amen." August lifted her head. "Now we may eat our dinner."

But when she uncovered her plate, August gulped. There was no meat, no chicken, no steak, no beef. Dinner was several different kinds of vegetables. She considered herself a carnivore; she couldn't go without meat for more than a day or two. Disgusted by the greens, August took a deep breath. The broccoli looked raw, the spinach was cooked with garlic, and the asparagus was chopped in half and boiled, which August didn't like. She poked at the broccoli with her fork. She did not feel like eating. This was a disaster. There wasn't even rice to go with the meal. She would have to be a herbivore for one day. At least there was dessert and beverages.

"What's wrong, August?" Carisie asked, looking worried.

"Nothing. Nothing at all." August placed a piece of broccoli into her mouth.

"August, my dear, in our world, we have rules and regulations too. We don't eat meat here, we are all vegetarians. That's rule number one. Rule number two: the animals around Camberdice must not be hunted. Rule number three: the animals are our best friends. They shall not be cast aside or abandoned. Rule number four: weapons can only be used under certain circumstances. For example, we don't use weapons on other people; we only use them to protect ourselves from the darkness. Rule number five, the most important one, is that we must look after each other." Carisie waited for August to reply.

"Yes, ma'am. I understand." August picked up her fork and reluctantly began to eat the vegetables. It wasn't an easy job, but she forced herself to do it. How she missed all the delicious food back on Earth: pizza with crispy crust, tender and juicy steak, smoked salmon. She shook off these thoughts and focused on her plate. She couldn't wait for dessert.

Meanwhile, Traise was enjoying her meal. She gulped down the broccoli, spinach, and asparagus with delight. Carisie was keeping an eye on August, making sure she finished all her food.

To August, it wasn't a pleasant meal, but she did not want to starve. After she had finished, she wiped her mouth with a lavender-scented napkin, put down her fork and knife, and waited.

"We may move on to dessert, chocolate cake," Carisie said.

The presentation of the cake was terrific. A red cherry sat on top of the buttercream frosting. A piece of marbled chocolate was placed at the side of the plate. Inside the cake was a thick layer of chocolate ganache with fresh rasberries. August eagerly dug her fork into the cake. The chocolate was rich and dark and melted in her mouth, and the cake was perfectly baked, thick and moist, not too sweet nor too bitter. It was so good that August imagined herself diving into a pool of chocolate ganache. The rasberries burst in her mouth, filling her mouth with both sweet and sour. She finished her serving in less than five minutes and waited for Carisie and Trasie to finish theirs.

"That cake was *so* nice," August praised. "There are no words for it. It was beyond perfect!"

"I'm happy that you liked it." Carisie smiled from ear to ear. She gently placed her fork on her plate. "Girls, would you like orange juice, apple juice, or watermelon juice?" she asked, offering the selection of juices.

"Watermelon juice, please," August replied.

"Orange juice, please, My Lady," Traise replied shyly.

Carisie lifted the pitcher of watermelon juice and poured it into August's purple glass. Then she then lifted the pitcher of orange juice and poured it into Traise's white glass.

"Thank you, My Lady. You're too kind," Traise said. She sipped her orange juice.

"Traise, how long have you been worked here?" August asked shyly.

"Ever since I was born."

"But where are your parents?"

"My parents are poor. They want me to have a better life here in the palace, so I don't have to worry about food and clothing."

"I'm really sorry. I shouldn't have asked."

"It's OK. I still see them once a mons."

"What's a *mons?*"

"Oh, er . . . it is one way we measure time. There are twelve mons in a year."

"Oh, *months* . . ."

"Is that how you say it on Earth? Camberdice is so different from Earth," Carisie said. "Magical creatures live here."

"What kind of creatures?"

"You'll explore for yourself soon. I don't want to spoil the surprise. Creatures here are beautiful and elegant. You'll see what I mean when you meet them."

"I can't wait!" August lifted her cup and sipped her watermelon juice. Sweet and full of pulp, it flowed smoothly down her throat and cooled her stomach. She finished her juice and wiped her mouth.

"Are you both finished?" Carisie asked them.

"Yes, all done," August replied, and Traise nodded. Without further conversation, they all rose from their seats. August bid Traise goodnight as she headed downstairs. Then August walked back to own her room with her mother.

THE GOODNIGHT SONG

"READY FOR A good night's sleep?" Carisie asked. She lowered the bedsheets and fluffed the pillow as August changed back into her pyjamas.

"Yeah, I'm tired." August rubbed her eyes and climbed into the soft, comforting bed.

Carisie opened the shuttered windows, grabbed a cushioned stool and settled down beside the bed, and put the box containing Paul's book on the bedside table. She brushed the hair off August's forehead and tucked it behind her ears and then pulled the blankets up over August's chest.

"I missed you so much. Now that you're back, I couldn't ask for anything more. When you were younger, I used to sing you a goodnight song." Carisie looked at August lovingly. It was called 'Good Night, My Love.'"

"I've heard that before on Earth. Could you sing it?"

"Anything for my one and only daughter." Carisie sat up tall and inhaled deeply. "Here goes . . . 'Good night, my one and only love, my life and my pride. You dream in your dreams; I hope the beautiful ones come true in life."

August recalled the dream she had had back home about the book devouring her. It had come true.

"'Someday you'll remember this song, oh, my one and only love, and you'll give it to your own children. Shake away your fear, my one and only love, shake away your insecurities, because I will always be there for my love." August drifted off to sleep.

A STAG OF HER OWN

THE MORNING SUN climbed in the cloudless sky and shone brightly across the land. Sunlight entered the room and stung August's eyes. She crawled out of bed and sat up on the end of it. She wondered what was happening at home on Earth. Were her parents worried about her? Were they OK? She looked over at the desk. There was a new piece of clothing lying on a wooden tray. Traise must have placed it there before the sun rose.

August picked up the dress. It was was a short, plain, cream-coloured dress. She slipped into it and looked in the mirror to see a purple-eyed girl in a beautiful dress. The back of it was cut in a V-shape to reveal her shoulders and back. She slipped her feet into her cream flats and waited for Traise.

Knock, knock, knock. When the maid finally arrived, August jumped off her bed and exited the room quickly. "Thanks for fetching me."

"No problem, it's my job. You look very beautiful in that dress," Traise said.

"Thank you. So where are we heading?"

"The paddock."

As August and Traise passed through the halls and down the stairs, guards bowed at August and greeted her in unison. August nodded shyly in return.

Outside, the morning sun beamed orange and yellow, brightening and warming the Earth. In the paddock, Carisie was riding the beautiful white stag August had seen grazing yesterday, the one with golden markings on its forehead. She was astonished by Carisie's elegance as she galloped across the field. Carisie's blonde hair swayed in the wind like a flag. When she spotted August, she halted her mount and trotted to the fence gracefully. Then she dismounted and opened the fence door. Once again, August was breathless as she admired the beautiful stag.

Carisie patted the stag's neck. "Thank you once again, Traise, and a very good morning to you, August. Meet Gloria, my mount."

August reached out and gently ran her palm over the creature's muzzle. "She's beautiful."

"Yes, indeed. And there at the far end is your stag." Carisie pointed to the moss-covered oak tree that stood to at one end of the paddock. Underneath its leafy branches stood a white stag. Its white antlers curved and branched, and golden markings wound around them. On its forehead was a golden sun, and on its left hindquarters was a golden rose-like marking the size of a palm.

"Wow" was all August said. She was overwhelmed by surprise, happiness, and excitement. August instantly fell in love with her stag. She couldn't have asked for more. It was perfect. She stepped over the grass which was mushy and covered in dew.

Carisie clicked her tongue, and August's stag cantered towards the goddess.

"Good boy!" Carisie rewarded the creature with a pat on the neck. It lowered its head to August and allowed her to pat its neck. "His name is Rafale. He's yours."

THE LEGEND OF THE
WHITE STAG

WHITE STAGS GALLOPED gracefully in the green field and devoured the grass beneath them, their coats glimmering under the beaming sun. Born with bravery and intelligence, they carried their riders with pride and were loyal to them. To protect its rider, a stag would walk over a bridge on fire or sacrifice itself by catching an arrow. Stags' antlers were tall and bold and could be used like sharp swords. Each stag was born with distinctive golden markings which made it unique. They loved their owners unconditionally.

AUGUST'S FIRST RIDE

CARISIE UNTIED A piece of rope from the fence and handed it to August, who looked at her mother with a confused expression. "Tie the rope around Rafale's neck," Carisie explained, "not too tight and not too loose." She stepped back to observe as August looped the rope around the creature's neck and tied a dead knot. "Five fingers should fit into the gap," Carisie instructed. August fitted five fingers into the gap between the stag's neck and the rope. "No, that's too loose. See, you can fit in an extra finger." Carisie assisted August in untying the knot. "Try it again." August tied the rope again and fitted five fingers into the gap. This time it fit better. "That's good for a second try. Now I'll teach you how to mount a stag."

Carisie placed both of her hands on her own stag's back and lifted herself off the ground. She swung her right leg gracefully over its back and sat up tall, squaring her shoulders. Gloria had stood rooted to the ground, not moving much while Carisie mounted. "Always mount on the left side. Now it's your turn."

August placed her hands on Rafale's back and pulled herself up. She lifted her right leg and swung it clumsily over the stag's broad back. Instead of sitting up, she slid too far over to the right and fell off his back. Rafale snorted and shook his head as if he were laughing at August. "Even the stag thinks it's funny," August said, laughing as she got to her feet.

"Be careful, my dear. You're not hurt, are you?" Carisie's face showed worry.

"No, it's not that bad." August brushed some dirt off her dress and returned to the left side of the stag.

"Try again. Be careful this time. Try to jump up and then lift your right leg."

August counted to three before jumping and lifting herself off the ground. This time, she got stuck halfway up in an awkward position. Carisie shooked her head and chuckled. "Again," she said, trying to hide her laughter.

August slid back to the ground. "Could I try a different way this time?" she asked.

"Sure, if it helps." Carisie smiled, her eyes crinkling.

August took a few steps back and took a deep breath. "Here I go!" She charged forward and jumped up to flop down across the stag's broad back. Then she lifted her right leg and slid it over. She sat up. Mission accomplished.

"Great job!" Carisie clapped her hands.

"I call that 'August's Belly-Flop.'" They both chuckled. August rewarded Rafale with a pat on the neck for not moving around when she had jumped onto his back. "What's next?"

Carisie picked up the rein with one hand and nudged Gloria forward. Then she stopped beside August. "Kick him lightly on the flank and he should move forward."

August kicked softly on Rafale's flank, and he began to walk. As he moved underneath her, August's hips rocked from side to side. Carisie kept pace with them. "Try to feel the rhythm."

August paid attention to the stag's coordinated movements: his right forelimb moved at the same time as his left hind leg, and his left forelimb moved with his right hind leg. "Great job!" Carisie praised.

"Now what? We're going to crash into the fence!" August exclaimed anxiously.

"Don't worry, we'll turn right soon," Carisie reassured. "Relax. He can tell that your muscles are tensed. Put your weight on your right leg and kick with your left leg."

August shifted her body weight over to her right foot and gently kicked the stag with her left foot. As if by magic, he turned and kept walking at an even pace.

"Now, I call that riding," Carisie said.

"I call that a *miracle!*" August joked. She patted the stag again. He kept walking straight along the fence. August enjoyed the morning breeze against her face as she rode. It was as fresh as peppermint.

"Now let's trot."

"Huh?" August was confused.

"Trotting is kind of like jogging," Carisie said. She nudged Gloria, who began to trot with long strides. Carisie stayed upright with her shoulders back. "Kick Rafale a little bit harder at his flank and prepare for trotting."

August kicked, and the stag responded immediately, trotting up alongside Gloria. August gasped nervously. As Rafale sped up, she started sliding to her right and to her left; she was terrified. She couldn't find Rafale's rhythm, and she was flopping all over the place.

"Find your balance!" Carisie shouted. "Square your shoulders and put all of your weight into your hips. Sit up straight so you don't fall, and feel the rhythm!"

August struggled but managed to follow Carisie's instructions. She put her shoulders back and squared her hips.

"You should feel like you're following the stag's movements," Carisie added.

August nodded and observed Rafale's movements. She kept her hips glued to her seat and finally managed to stay on her mount without flopping around. She was *riding*.

"Found your rhythm?" Carisie asked.

"Yes! When he moves his legs once, I bounce once. When he moves his legs twice, I bounce twice," August answered with confidence.

Carisie smiled and nodded. "Yes, you are dead right." Then she pulled on the rein so that Gloria stopped.

"How do you stop?" August asked. "I'm gonna go on and on forever!"

"Pull the rein and lean backwards. Don't fall off!"

August leaned backwards and pulled the rein tightly with her hand. Rafale stopped and stumbled a few steps.

"That's good, but try to pull and lean at the same time. He stumbled after you stopped him—he shouldn't be doing that."

August nodded and nudged her stag forward. Her heart thumped loudly as he moved beneath her. She couldn't believe that she was riding such a majestic creature. Back on Earth, she had never really felt that she belonged. Now, she felt comfort being around the people here and for once, she felt . . . normal. August caught up with Carisie and smiled broadly at her. She wondered if her mother felt proud of her.

"You did a great job for your time riding," Carisie said. "Again, trot!"

August nudged Rafale into a trot and squared her shoulders. Everything felt right. She was following the stag's movement, her hips stayed on his back, and her shoulders were square. The cold, fresh breeze blew through her loose hair. She felt free.

"And . . . stop!" Carisie ordered. She halted her mount and waited for August to do the same.

August counted to three and pulled the rein while leaning backwards at the same time. Rafale stopped and stood still, waiting for August's next command.

"That's much better." Carisie dismounted by lifting her right leg and swinging it over to the left. Then she landed smoothly on the ground. As Carisie untied Gloria, August wondered for the thousandth time how her mother could be so perfect in everything she did. "Do the same as I did," Carisie instructed. "Just lift your right leg and swing it over."

August tried her best to not mess up. She swung her leg over and landed harshly on the ground. Once she landed, she felt the soreness in her legs. Her muscles were aching, her ankles bruised. She released Rafale and walked towards her mother, who was waiting by the fence. Struggling to move in spite of her pain, she walked like a penguin.

Carisie patted her arm. "You were very good for your first ride."

"Thank you. I really enjoyed that."

"Feeling a little sore?"

"Yeah."

"It will hurt for a while. Take a nice, warm bath when you reach your room. We'll meet Matt at three."

August nodded, ignoring the pain attacking her limbs, and moved forward.

A Sore Afternoon

Agust stepped painfully into her room. She hurried into the bathroom and drew a warm bath. It wasn't as relaxing as she'd hoped, however. The pain remained, and a huge bruise was coming up on her left ankle. When she was finished, she exited the bathroom. The scent of lavender escaped into her room, filling the space with a sweet aroma.

On her bed lay another dress. She picked it up and examined its details. It had a low V-neck and long lace sleeves. She slipped into the dress and was shocked to see herself in the mirror. She had never in her life worn anything as revealing as this. She did look good in it. The dress wrapped around her waist, showing her curves. For the first time, she willingly combed her hair. She tied it into a neat braid and admired her own work. For once, she felt pretty. She walked around the room, dragging the dress's train across the carpet.

Knock, knock, knock. August answered the door expecting Traise. It turned out to be her mother.

"Oh, my goodness, you look incredibly beautiful!" Carisie exclaimed, turning August around. August noticed Carisie's long, elegant cream-and-gold dress.

"You too! Flawless, as usual."

Carisie showed August the new shoes she'd brought and placed them on the floor. August slipped her sore feet into the flats and reached for Carisie's hand. Mother and daughter walked together through the palace.

Three Stags

When they walked out the front door, August saw three stags waiting patiencely under the afternoon sun. She spotted her stag, Rafale, on the right, and Carisie's stag, Gloria, in the middle. She did not recognize the stag on the left. It had a golden rose-like marking on its shoulder.

August walked towards her stag with confidence, reaching out to stroke his forehead. She traced her fingers along the golden sun marking on his forehead. Rafale rested his muzzle on August's shoulder. She placed her cheek against his and looked into his purple eye. It reflected the silhoutte of a strong, beautiful girl. *Purple eyes . . . just like mine,* she thought.

August heard footsteps coming from behind. It was Matt.

"Wow," he blurted out.

"What? What's wrong?" August frowned at Matt.

"Nothing, you just look different today." He looked away quickly.

"In a good way or a bad way?"

"In a beautiful way," he said.

August felt a rush of heat conquering her cheeks. She was blushing. "Well, thank you," she replied shyly. She patted Rafale's neck, hiding from Matt's handsome blue eyes.

"All right, lovebirds, it's time to mount," Carisie joked. She handed ropes to August and Matt.

August tossed the rope around Rafale's neck and knotted it. She didn't want to embarrass herself in front of Matt, so she prayed that it was correctly tied. She fitted five fingers into the gap—perfect. She exhaled in relief and flopped onto her stag.

When everybody was mounted, Carisie led the way along the stone path. The three of them walked side by side and remained silent as they passed the fountain. Just before they reached the gate, Carisie broke the silence.

"How old are you, Matt?"

"I'm fourteen years old."

"And with whom do you live?"

"With my parents and my little sister."

"Do we have permission to visit them today?"

"Yes, of course! You're the goddess. My family will be very happy to meet you."

August could tell Carisie was trying to keep things from being awkward for her and Matt.

The guards at the gate bowed and opened it for them. August could barely contain her excitement. She was eager to explore the land she had come from and to which she belonged. For the first time, she stopped thinking about her Earth parents. She felt the rein in her hand and wondered, *What is out there waiting for me?* There was so much more to learn, so much to discover. It was unreal: she was living in a place where magic really did exist. She closed her eyes and felt Rafale's shoulders move underneath her.

She hummed a tune, and the white birds joined in, turning what had been silence into music. The sky was clear. The sun hung high among the aspen trees, and their shadows followed them, long and dark.

They rode over hills and through rivers. August felt the rush of river water flowing over her feet as Rafale walked slowly and steadily across riverbeds, trying to avoid rocks and pebbles. He knew that his job was to protect August.

Sweat streamed down August's forehead. She was tired. Every single one of her muscles ached. As soon as she spotted the silhouttes of houses, she jumped down from her seat.

"Oh, thank goodness! We're there!" she yelped, relieved.

"August, this is the village of Camberdice."

"What are we waiting for? Trot ahead!" August kicked Rafale, and he broke into a trot. The other two followed behind, and soon, they reached the village's entrance, where a sign that read "Village of Camberdice" hung high above them. She halted Rafale and looked around the town.

THE VILLAGE OF CAMBERDICE

Village of Camberdice had only one street with houses and cottages on either side. A sound echoed in the street: *clip clop, clip clop*. August saw a horse cart coming towards them; two horses were harnessed to a black buggy. Carisie allowed Matt to lead the way.

When they rode into the asphalt road, the villagers all stopped what they were doing and bowed at Carisie. An old woman stared at August in disbelief. "People, this is Carisa! The lost child of Camberdice has returned!" The people started to cheer. They swarmed towards her. "She is the lost child. Her eyes prove it!" one said. "She really is the lost child. I can't believe it!" another exclaimed. "She is a beauty just like her mother," said a lady.

The situation overwhelmed August. She didn't know what to do or say. She just sat quietly on her stag and forced herself to smile. A dun horse and rider passed by; the rider lowered his head and saluted as he left the crowd.

Carisie seemed to sense the uneasiness in August. She lifted her hand. "It's time for us to move on. Thank you for the welcome. We appreciate it." The people moved off and returned to their work.

Matt, Carisie, and August continued on. A horse with a wooden cart rattled past. A rider on a bay stallion trotted by. The village was full of horses. Everybody had their own. A little boy groomed his yearling while a girl watered hers. A tall man slipped a halter onto his horse's head while his wife prepared it a bucket of mash. The sweet smell of oats entered August's lungs. She suddenly remembered the *Legend of Two Lands*, which told that Carisie, the goddess of the wind, had invited equines to live in the land. That explained all the equines in Camberdice.

Matt led them down the street and around a corner; then he stopped in front of a house and dismounted. "This is my house. Please, come inside."

Carisie dismounted effortlessly. August lifted her right leg and was hit by all of her soreness and pain at once. She would be so embarrassed if she got stuck on her mount again. Matt must have realized that she was in trouble, because he ran towards her and took her by the waist to help her down. She blushed again. "Thanks."

"No problem at all." Matt led the way to his house. August took her mother's hand and they followed.

Beside the house, three horses were grazing freely and a little girl was playing with her Shetland pony's mane. "Hi, Matty! Who are your friends?" she asked curiously.

"The goddess and her daughter, my dear."

"Wow, they sure are pretty."

"Yes, indeed. Where's Mom?"

"In the kitchen."

MATT'S HOUSE

THE DÉCOR INSIDE the house was simple. The walls and ceiling were white. A painting of the three goddesses hung on the wall beside a small picture of Matt's family. Matt invited Carisie and August to sit down on the couch and went to look for his mother in the kitchen. August examined the family picture. There was Matt as a little blue-eyed boy. Behind them, the mother was wearing a burgundy dress and the father was wearing a white tuxedo.

Then Matt came back in, followed by his mother. She was wearing a simple navy-blue dress, and her black hair flowed down her shoulders. She appeared stunned to see them. "Good evening." She bowed and brought over a tray with cups of freshly brewed chrysanthemum tea. "I'm honoured to meet you. My name is Chaise."

"Thank you. The privilege is mine," Carisie said. Smiling, she turned to introduce August. "This is my daughter, the lost child of Camberdice. She was found by your son. You should be very proud of him. I owe you both many thanks."

"There's no need to thank us. He was just doing what was supposed to be done. I must say that your daughter is a beautiful young woman. She is destined to be just like her parents."

"Thanks." August placed her cup onto the table just as Matt's sister barged in, sobbing.

"*I can't tie a braid!*" she cried at the top of her lungs.

Chaise ran to her and put her arms around the girl. "I'll come help you as soon as possible, all right?" she said soothingly. But the girl continued to cry.

"No! I want it now!" Tears streamed down her rosy cheeks.

August came over and patted the girl on the head. "I'll help you, OK?" She pinched the girl's cheek and made her laugh.

"OK." The little girl dried her tears. August picked her up and carried her outside, where the pony was waiting quietly for his little master to return. The girl jumped down and patted the pony; then she pointed to his tail. "I can't tie a braid. Can you please help me?" She looked up at August with gigantic, watery eyes.

"Sure, but first you have to tell me your name."

"You can call me Kristy."

"All right then, Kristy." August began to braid the pony's tail, showing Kristy what to do as she moved her fingers through the bushy hair. "First you separate the hair into three strands. Then you cross one over the other, like this." She crossed the leftmost strand over the middle one, then the rightmost strand over the middle one. "Get it?" Kristy nodded as she watched carefully. "Done!"

"Thank you, big girl. You're the best!" Kristy smiled broadly and hugged August's leg.

August laughed. "You're a cute one." She picked Kristy up and brought her inside. Carisie, Chaise, and Matt seemed to have been having an enjoyable chat.

"Oh, my dear, I wish you the best," Chaise said to Carisie.

August didn't know what they were talking about, and she wasn't really interested. She had had a great time with Kristy, her muscles were still aching from the morning's training, and now the sun was setting.

Carisie and August bid the family farewell and then went outside to mount their stags. Matt's stag followed behind without reins. He knew he had to follow them in order to get home, and he behaved very well. August was amazed by the stag's intelligence. As they rode home, the sun turned orange-red and dyed the clouds a dark orange. A flock of letter doves flew above them, flapping their strong wings as they raced across the sky.

SWEET STRAWBERRIES

AT THE PALACE, they went into the dining room, where dinner was already laid out on the table. August forced herself to eat her vegetables, looking forward to dessert. This time, it was a bowl of bright-red strawberries, fresh, juicy, and sweet. She sipped watermelon juice and munched on strawberries until they were gone. Then she excused herself for bed.

Through the bedroom window, August saw the moon climbing the starry sky. It shone silver, spreading its light across the land. She let out a loud yawn and climbed into her comfortable bed, wondering what tomorrow would bring.

HILL CAMBERDICE

A BEAM OF GOLDEN sunlight settled on August's face, waking her. She didn't feel like getting up. The soreness in her muscles lingered; the pain had not decreased. She struggled to find her strength. She had to get up before her mother came for her. She pulled herself up and dragged her bruised legs across the sheet. *I need a wheelchair*, she thought.

She limped over to the tray on the desk that held her new cream-coloured dress for the day, picked it up, and slipped into it. She finger-combed her hair and waited a long fifteen minutes before hearing a knock on the door. She slipped into her flats and opened the door to find Traise there.

"Good morning, My Lady."

"Quit it with the 'Lady'. Just call me August." They walked through the halls and down the winding staircase.

"You'll be riding today, August." Traise opened the front door for August. Outside, Gloria and Rafale stood before her, swishing their tails in rhythm.

"Is Matt coming today?"

"I'm sorry, I don't know," Traise said as she took her leave.

"Good morning, my dear." Carisie took August by the hand and led her over to Rafale. "There is a surprise is waiting for you."

August flopped onto Rafale and held the rein in her hand. She nudged him forward and followed her mother on Gloria. They rode slowly to enjoy the the loud chirping of the birds and the rows of aspen trees rattling in the morning breeze.

Finally, Carisie started a conversation. "Hill Camberdice is a hill that dominates the land. It stands tall and bold, strong and sturdy."

"And?" August could tell something was waiting for her there.

"You'll see for yourself." Carisie pointed to a tall, grassy hill in the distance. "There it is." Then she broke into a trot.

August followed, squaring her shoulders and trying to stay with the stag's movement. Her muscles hurt, her arms hurt, her heels hurt—pratically everything hurt. She had never thought that riding would be as difficult as what she was experiencing. They were on a steep, winding path up the top of the hill. August felt gravity pulling her downwards and felt a little scared. She was placing all of her trust in Rafale. One slip might cause their death. But the white stag continued bravely, bracing against the trail.

The air became colder as they got higher. Finally, August saw that the ground flattened out; they had reached the top of the hill. She breathed the scent of grass deep into her lungs. Beautiful wildflowers spread over the ground, dotting the green surface with yellow and white.

"Now just wait and see," Carisie said mysteriously and looked upwards.

THE PEGASUS

August saw something flying above them, something big and wide with flapping wings. Through the cottony clouds, their silhoutte of the creature—the creatures—was only partially visible. One of them dove through the clouds, its wings flat against its back. August couldn't take her eyes off it. She was desperate to know what these magical creatures were. It plunged down and landed on its hooves. August gasped. She couldn't believe her eyes. The creature stood at sixteen hands. It spread its giant white wings and closed them again, folding them at its sides.

"A pegasus . . ." She dismounted Rafale and stood silently watching the pegasus for a few moments. Then she gathered her courage and walked slowly and calmly towards the winged stallion. She looked into his eyes and could see his bravery and wisdom. She reached out her hand and placed it softly onto the pegasus's nose. Her body tingled and her hands trembled. She wondered if she were still asleep and this was all a dream. If it was, she didn't want it to end.

THE LEGEND OF THE PEGASUS

Pegasuses were majestic white horses born with white fur coats, huge white wingss, and thick manes that flowed like ocean waves. They were born with bravery and courage—they were fearless. They mounted the clouds, strong and bold. Their spirits were unbreakable. Chasing the wind and racing with eagles, they settled on Hill Camberdice. There they were close to humans, and they loved them. If you flew with a pegasus, you tasted the joy of freedom and would never forget the journey that you'd shared.

A Flight with the Pegasus

More winged horses landed on the hill one by one, surrounding August. Their hooves plunged deep into the dirt. They galloped and bolted and stretched their strong legs. But the first stallion did not move. Instead, he continued to stand quietly before August and leaned his cheek against hers. August knew he liked her. She patted his shoulder and felt pounds of lean muscle.

Nearby, Carisie mounted a pegasus. August knew the only one she would try to mount was the one standing before her, the one that had allowed her to pat his nose. She flopped across his broad back and lifted her leg over. The distance between her and the ground was huge; the stallion was so tall.

"Hold on to his mane!" Carisie shouted. "Lean against his neck!" Without further words, she lifted off the hill.

"OK, buddy. We can do this." August gave the stallion a kick, and he charged off into a gallop. He took six strides and took off, flapping his broad white wings. August tasted the wind in her mouth and felt free. She held on to the pegasus's mane and leaned forward against his neck. The wind pushed against her cheeks and ran through her hair. She looked around the cloudless blue sky. What had happened to the clouds? She looked down and saw them clustered underneath them. They had flown even higher than she had thought. She caught a glimpse of Carisie and chased after her.

"This is fun!" August shouted.

"Follow me!" Carisie charged forward. Her pegasus climbed higher. She headed for a thick white cloud and slowed him down. The pegasus landed on the cloud and closed his wings. Carisie slipped off his back and beckoned to August.

"Are you nuts? You're standing on a cloud!" August shouted.

"Trust me, August, you won't fall."

"I don't want to die so young."

"You won't!"

"How do you even do that? You're freaking me out!"

"The cloud is thick enough for us to stand on."

"What? We can't do that back on Earth!"

"Camberdice is far different from Earth. There is magic here that doesn't exist on Earth."

"How can I trust you?"

"You're my daughter," Carisie said, laughing. "I won't kill you."

"OK, fine." August guided her pegasus onto the cloud. It took her awhile to find the courage to dismount. She slipped off the pegasus's back, still clinging to his thick mane just in case.

"Let go, August. You won't fall. Trust me and you'll have one of the best experiences of your life."

August thought thrice before releasing her fingers and warily moving moved away from the pegasus. It felt as though she were standing on a solid surface, but she was standing on a cloud—a cloud! She jumped and felt the cloud bounce like a spring mattress. "This is so cool! I could stay here forever!"

"Do you want to ride it?"

"How?"

"With wind." Carisie opened her arms and recited a spell. A gust of wind came towards them and drove the cloud forward. They were travelling across the sky. August spotted a flock of letter doves ahead of them.

"What if I fell? What would happen?"

"Some other clouds would catch you."

"What if there weren't any?"

"Then I would save you."

"How?"

"With wind." Carisie put her arm around August's shoulders. "Are you cold?"

August shook her head and turned her head towards her mother. "No, not at all, Mom."

Carisie looked stunned. "You called me 'Mom'. That's the first time you've called me that since before you went missing." She held August tightly and smiled brightly. "It warms my heart. It really does."

August trusted Carisie and she loved her—she was certain that she did. She pressed her cheek to Carisie's chest and enjoyed the scenery around them. Houses and moors passed below them. She could see Candrale, white and shiny. She patted her pegasus and looked into his eyes.

"What's his name?" she asked.

"They don't have names, but you can give him one if you want to."

August thought hard. "Storm. I'll call him Storm." She patted his and ran her fingers through his thick, wavy mane.

"Shall we go down now?" Carisie asked.

August nodded and climbed onto Storm. She kicked and he dove down through the blurry clouds, his wings laid flat against his back. She held tightly to his mane as he plunged through the cloud layers. This was better than a roller-coaster ride at Universal Studios, better than Disney World. She closed her eyes against the cool wind.

THE PEGASUS FOALS

As THEY GOT closer to the ground, August's heart thumped loudly in her chest. She closed her eyes as the pegasus landed and bumped against his neck. She couldn't find words to describe the flight. It had been too wonderful for words. Carisie landed beside her and dismounted expertly. She was trained as a warrior, a hunter, and a leader.

Little pegasus foals roamed the top of the hill, their fluffy little wings hanging at their sides. One foal flapped its wings and reared up on its hind legs. Another one bolted and galloped. They chased each other's tails. August held her breath as she dismounted Storm. It was harder than it looked when Carisie did it because the pegasus was so tall. She swung her leg back, slid off his broad back, and fell to the ground.

The pegasus foals ran towards her and licked at her arms. She patted their tiny withers, got to her feet, and walked towards her mother.

"Where are we going now?"

"We're going home." Carisie replied.

August searched for the stags, but they were nowhere to be found. "Where are Gloria and Rafale?"

"Hold on, they'll come soon." Carisie whistled. After a second, the ground rumbled. The stags cantered towards them from a distance and slowed to a trot as they got closer.

Carisie mounted Gloria and August belly-flopped onto Rafale. They rode peacefully together, enjoying the breathtaking scenery as they travelled down the sloping hill.

An Exciting Night

August retired to bed after finishing her dinner of more greens and broccoli. She settled her heavy head on the soft pillow and closed her eyes. She turned herself over and tried to get comfortable, but her aching muscles didn't feel any better. She counted to a hundred but still couldn't fall asleep, even though she was very tired. Her heart beat loud and fast, and her mind raced at the speed of light. She couldn't contain the excitement of the day. If she had ridden a pegasus today, what was waiting for her tomorrow? She rubbed her eyes. She had to get to sleep before sunrise, before the next adventure arrived.

Finally, after what felt like years of restlessly turning and shifting, August fell soundly asleep.

THE LAVENDER FIELD

Aᴜɢᴜsᴛ ᴡᴏᴋᴇ ᴀs the sun rose. She cast aside her blanket and got up groggily. She changed into the new dress and combed her hair. In the mirror, she saw that her purple eyes gleamed in the sunlight and her lips were pinkish red like a water-lily. Her dress glowed silver and white. Carisie entered the room holding a barrette shaped like a white bow. She sat August down on a cushioned stool and ran her fingers through August's golden hair.

"Let me do your hair." Carisie waterfall-braided August's smooth hair, tied the end with a piece of horsehair, and then clipped the barrette onto the braid. She stepped back to admire her work and asked August to stand up and twirl. "Perfect! A piece of fine art." She clasped her hands together and showed August the braid in the mirror.

"It's beautiful!" August said.

"You're beautiful," Carisie responded. "Let's go." Carisie led the way through the halls of paintings and statues and came to the marble staircase.

August held the railing with one hand and her mother's hand with the other. Carisie's palm was warm and soft. Her fingers were long and delicate. August felt happy and excited. They exited the front door and saw their mounts waiting, swishing their tails in rhythm.

August released her mother's hand and walked over to Rafale. A guard gave her a rope, which she tossed over the stag's neck and then tied carefully, checking that five fingers fit underneath. She flopped onto Rafale's back to mount, sat up straight, and nudged Rafale into a walk. She was starting to understand his movements and his gait and the feeling of his transitions between walking and trotting.

Carisie mounted Gloria and dusted a piece of straw of her right antler. August wondered what awaited her today. They walked past the rows of aspen trees and exited the grounds of Candrale.

"August, there are three goddesses in Camberdice," Carisie explained. "Oakastine is the goddess of the woods, Meraida is the goddess of the water, and I am the goddess of the wind. We each have our own palace. Candrale is mine, Oakrale is Oakastine's, and Merale is Meraida's. We work together to bring water, wind, and crops to the land. Today we will meet Oakastine, goddess of the woods."

August tried to absorb as much information as possible.

"The other goddesses of Camberdice are my close allies. We fight together, and we will need your help, August."

"For what?"

"As I said earlier, the Son of Earth will soon attack this land. The last glow that your father cast won't last forever. You are still young, so the glow that you cast will also be weak, but it will be enough to delay the eclipse."

"So, you're telling me that I have to fight him."

"Yes. Unfortunately, the goddesses can't help you," Carisie said. "You will be your own saviour as well as ours. When the eclipse strikes, we will lose our only light, the sun. Then we will be unable to cast any spells or to use our powers, so we won't be able to help much. But you were born with the sun. You will still have power.

"But you still have to fight him with your own hands," she continued. The darkness is powerful. You will need intense training. I can't predict when the darkness will occur, but I can tell you that it will happen soon. I want you to be prepared. I don't want to lose you."

August gulped. "Do I have to kill him?"

"You don't have to, but you can destroy him."

"Isn't that the same thing?"

"No. In Camberdice, killing invloves spilling blood, while destroying banishes evil."

"So I still have to fight him."

"Yes, you do, but I will watch you from above and pray for you. I will teach you to be a hunter and a warrior. For now, time is our only enemy."

August nodded in response but remained silent. She tried to dismiss her uneasiness and focus on the path. After a few minutes, they reached a field covered in purple flowers.

"It's a lavender field." Carisie entered the field.

The tall plants reached up the stags' withers. The fragrant lavender scented the air around them. August took a deep breath and exhaled. She could taste the sweetness of the air. She leaned down to her left and ran her fingers through the purple flowers; then she plucked one and placed it on one of Rafale's antlers.

"A flower to mark my stag," she said to her mother. They trotted across the purple field and entered a forest.

THE WOODS

As they walked deeper into the forest, the light grew dimmer. The path was darker because the tree branches grew inwards, blocking out the sunlight. The trees were covered in moss, and their leaves were dark green. August yelped when she saw a dark-green tarantula the size of a fist crawling up a tree trunk.

"Calm down, it's only a spider," said Carisie. "They are friendly."

"No way! I hate, hate, *mega*-hate them."

Carisie chuckled.

August stayed close beside Carisie throughout the ride. She heard a hiss and turned to her left to see a dark-emerald bush viper wrapping itself around a tree trunk. It had dark-green slit-shaped pupils, and its body was covered in ridged scales. She jumped and screamed, terrified.

"It's OK, August dear, the snake is friendly." Carisie patted her daughter's trembling shoulder and took her hand.

"I don't like this forest at all! Snakes and spiders are friendly? You've got to be kidding me. They bite! It's in their nature."

"No, the creatures that live in Camberdice never bite, and that includes spiders and snakes."

"I never, ever want to touch one."

"Well then, I'm afraid that you will have to." Carisie reached over and picked up the viper. It wound itself around her arm and let out a sharp hiss. August shuddered in disgust as her mother handled the snake. "Hold it," Carisie said, bringing the viper close to August. "Lesson number one: you have to face your fear."

August gulped and stretched her hand out to her mother's, and the snake wriggled onto her shaking hand. August held her breath as the snake settled on her arm. She could feel its sleek skin on her own. "Wow," she whispered. She realized that anything was possible in Camberdice—*anything*. She watched the snake in silent awe for about fifteen minutes. Then her mother placed it back where it belonged and they continued on their journey.

THE UNICORNS

T HEY RODE FOR hours until at last they entered a clearing. August saw horse-like creatures grazing. Their coats were white dappled with silver, and their manes flowed and glowed silver and gold. A stallion raised its front legs and neighed; a mare cantered across the clearing. And they had pointy horns that shone brightly in the dark. August stared at the herd. *Unicorns.*

A stallion trotted around the clearing with his neck arched, carrying his tail proudly. His horn glowed, and his mane was long and wavy. August could tell he was spirited. He halted and stamped his hoof in the dirt, sending dust into the air.

August was astonished by the divine creature that stood before her. She looked at Carisie with wide eyes.

Carisie nodded. "Go ahead. You want to ride that stallion there, I can tell." She smiled. "Go, roam free."

August dismounted Rafale and walked calmly towards the horned stallion, clicking her tongue as she got closer. The stallion's ears twitched forward as she got closer. She gently stroked his muzzle. He blinked, and August saw her own reflection in his gleaming eyes.

THE LEGEND OF THE UNICORNS

Unicorns were equines closely related to horses and pegasuses. They had horns that glowed brightly in the dark, long and wavy manes, and strong and muscular legs. They trotted proudly through the green forest, curving their necks and carrying their tails high. Their hooves bit into the ground, sending clouds of dust up into the air. They were beautiful, elegant, friendly, and loving.

THE UNICORN RIDE

AUGUST RAN HER hand over the stallion's strong back and belly-flopped onto it. He stood seventeen hands tall. She took hold of his mane and felt its soft, smooth texture. Then she nudged him in the belly. He began to walk slowly. She felt his shoulders moving and his croup rising and falling under her. She wanted to go faster, so she kicked harder, and the stallion broke into a trot. He lifted his legs and bent his knees, curved his crest, and elegantly carried his tail up high. August bounced once but found her balance. She squared her shoulders and straightened her back and followed the movement of the unicorn.

August breathed deeply. She felt different: stronger, in control, and *normal*. She decided to stop and pulled on the stallion's mane, leaning backwards at the same time. Her heart pounded faster. The stallion slowed to a walk and stopped. August could feel his heart beating in his chest; gradually, their heartbeats synchronized. She felt a strong bond between them. She leaned forward and patted his shoulder, then dismounted, landing harshly on the ground. She wasn't a good rider—she admitted it.

Carisie urged Gloria forwards and patted the unicorn's back. "Let's go. Hop on your mount."

August clicked her tongue, and Rafale responded immediately, walking over to her. She mounted him, and they carried on with their journey.

A BRIGHTER PLACE

THE PATH GREW brighter; the trees became fewer and less dense. A speck of sunlight filtered through the leaves. August squinted. The sunlight was sharp and stung her eyes. Eventually the trees thinned out entirely, and they were in a green field, directly under the sun, which hung high in the bright-blue sky.

In the distance stood a tall, dominating palace. The trees behind them shook, and the leaves rattled. August could feel that something was coming. She shrieked and shortened her rein, ready to bolt.

"Shh . . . don't worry. She just likes a grand entrance, as always," Carisie reassured. She pointed into the sky. A flying creature sailed through the air, flapping its giant wings and circling the woods.

August tensed, afraid. The creature circled again, spitting flames out of its mouth. She clenched her fingers into a fist, her heart pounding.

"Calm down," Carisie said calmly. "It won't hurt you."

THE FROST DRAGON

THE WINGED CREATURE dashed down towards the ground, its wings spread wide. It leaned to the left and turned, eyes fixed on August. Then, with a loud thud, it landed right in front of her. August stumbled back, afraid. The ground shook, and a cloud of dust blew up around the creature. It flared its nostrils and produced a plume of smoke.

The dragon was at least forty feet long and fifteen feet tall. Its sharp claws dug deep into the dirt. Its gleaming eyes were light blue, and its pupils were black slits. Frost-blue spiky scales and an arrowhead-shaped tail covered its body like an armor.

A lady in a green gown sat boldly on the dragon's back. She dismounted by climbing down its spikes like a ladder and patted its shoulder. "Hello, Carisie," she greeted. "I see you brought someone with you."

"Good morning, Oakastine. I thought you would remember her."

"Wait a minute . . ." The lady looked closely at August's eyes and gasped. "Your lost child!"

"Yes, indeed."

"Oh, my goodness, she's back!" Oakastine leaned forward and hugged August tightly. "Carisa! You're back!"

"Hello, My Lady. It's a privilege to meet you. Please call me August," she said.

"Oh. Well, August, my dear, would you like to visit my palace?"

"Yes, please!"

"All right, then. Let's go to Oakrale on my dragon."

But August was terrified of the creature. Carisie wrapped her arm around her and led her closer to the frost dragon.

"She won't bite. Pat her," Carisie commanded. "Remember lesson one?"

August nodded. "Face your fear," she replied. She reached a hand out towards the dragon's face until she felt its scales underneath her palm. She patted it and looked into its eyes. Unexpectedly, August saw kindness and love there. The dragon wasn't dangerous at all! She was tame, and she loved her human friends.

Oakastine mounted the dragon. "Hop on!"

August carefully climbed up the dragon's spikes. Carisie sat behind August and held her tightly. The dragon rose up from the ground and blasted off into the sky.

August felt terrible for having judged the dragon. This truly had been a lesson.

THE LEGEND OF THE
FROST DRAGON

THE FROST DRAGON carried the goddess of the woods. Her skin was frost blue and covered in scales and spikes. She was furious and strong as she sailed across the sky, flapping her giant wings. She breathed fire and protected her owner under any circumstances. She was known to be a fearless creature with a kind heart.

A Roller-Coaster Ride

"WHOA!" AUGUST SCREAMED. "She's going so fast!"

"Not at all, this is her slowest speed," Oakastine shouted. "Do you want to go faster?"

"No—"

"Let's go!" The dragon flew even faster, flapping its wings rapidly.

"OMG, I think I'm gonna puke!" August closed her eyes for a moment and tried to control her fluttering stomach. Her heart beat wildly through her chest.

"Hang on, we're almost there," Okastine announced. The dragon dove down.

The strong wind currents pushed against August's cheeks. Tears filled her eyes. She felt her heart falling down to her stomach.

"We're landing now," Oakastine said. The dragon spread its wings and tilted left. They were getting really close to the ground now.

"I can't watch!" August screamed. She covered her face. They landed harshly onto the ground, sending dirt and grass flying in all directions. August sighed in relief and clasped her hands together. "It's over!" She climbed down from the dragon's back. Her face was as white as paper. She dramatically got down on the grass on her hands and knees as if she were hugging the ground. "Land! Oh, I missed you so much!"

Carisie and Oakastine chuckled and helped her back up. "You sure are a cheeky one," Oakastine said, winking at August.

"I agree," Carisie said. She patted August's head. "Say goodbye to the dragon for now."

August patted the creature's forehead. "Goodbye! I really do like you, I promise. I hope you like me too." She leaned forward and kissed the dragon's cheek. The dragon closed her eyes, seeming to enjoy the embrace, and then opened her eyes again. The clear, thin membranes that protected her eyes slid away, exposing her slit-shaped pupils. August waved and followed the goddesses.

FULL OF TREES

AUGUST WALKED WITH her mother and Oakastine through a garden full of dark-green roses and daisies in full bloom. Guarding the palace door was a white statue of a dragon with its mouth wide open to show razor-sharp teeth. They walked through the grand door.

Inside, trees grew from the walls and ceilings. The entire palace was covered in plants. August touched the bark of a tree and spotted a dark-emerald wasp spider beside her hand. This time, instead of screaming, she picked up the spider and allowed it to crawl on her hand. August now understood that the only way to defeat fear was to face it.

"Very good, August. You learn fast," Carisie said approvingly.

They walked through hall after hall and finally into a dining room. This room, too, was full of trees. The table was made out of maple wood and the chairs were tree stumps. Oakastine invited her guests to sit down and then whistled. A white martial eagle came flying in and landed on her shoulder. She clapped her hands, and several chefs entered. They placed dishes on the wooden table and then left the room.

"Please enjoy," Oakastine said, gesturing for them to begin dining.

August tried to inspect Oakastine's eyes without staring. They were dark green, different from hers and Carisie's eyes. Her hair, too, was dark green. The eagle observed August curiously and then flew away.

August removed the wooden cover and looked at her plate. It was even worse than she had expected. The plate was full of uncooked leaves and grasses; they weren't even boiled. August gulped and played with her food. She saw her mother looking at her with a warning expression. August placed a leaf in her mouth and chewed it. She tried to look as normal as possible, remembering some acting tips her drama teacher had once given her. She swallowing the leaf, smiled faintly, and drank deeply from her cup of water.

"Do you like it?" Oakastine asked, finishing her last strand of grass.

"Yes, I love it!" August faked a bright smile and placed another piece of leaf in her mouth. *I guess I'll be a horse for a day,* she thought.

After dinner, Oakastine sat up straight and crossed her arms on the table. August knew something imporatant was coming up.

"So, August, has your mother told you about the Son of Earth?"

August nodded.

"Do you know that you're our only hope?"

"Yes."

"Unfortunately, we don't have much time, my dear."

"I know."

"Please, August. You must save Camberdice, not only for us, but also for the sake of Earth."

"I understand."

"Do you know why you're the chosen one?"

"I was born with the sun."

"And why does that matter?"

"Only the sun can defeat the darkness."

"You're right. You carry a huge responsibility, my dear. I understand that it's hard, but please try to do your best."

"I will."

A Conference

Oakastine instructed one of the guards to take August on a tour of the palace, leaving the two goddesses alone in the tree-filled room. Carisie could see in Oakastine's face that she was worried.

"What are you afraid of?"

"Your child."

"Why so?" Carisie's eye narrowed.

"I'm afraid that she's too weak," Oakastine said, shaking her head.

"She's not!"

"But she's just a child." Oakastine said doubtfully.

"That may be, but her capabilities are beyond what I expected."

"What makes you say that?"

"She's very closely connected with the equines. They come after her."

"But what if . . . what if she is too weak for the battle?"

"I swear on my throne that she will be the one who saves us. I gurantee it," Carisie insisted. She leaned closer, waiting for her friend's answer.

"Don't make a promise that you can't keep."

"You know me. I keep all my promises."

"All right. Then train her well. The fate of the land is now in her hands."

"And I will not lose her again." Carisie slammed her fist on the table and rose from her seat.

She walked towards the door, inhaled deeply, and put on a smile. She opened the door and saw August standing with the guard, gazing through a small window at the green forest. Carisie's heart ached at August's innocence. She herself wasn't confident about the upcoming battle, but she had faith in her daughter.

"August dear, come in now," she said softly.

A Dragon's Tooth

August sat back down on her stump beside Carisie and placed her hands in her laps. Oakastine pushed a box across the table towards August. "It's a gift from me," she said, smiling pleasantly.

Inside the box was a tooth. Its edge was sharp enough to cut fabric. August picked it up and examined it.

"It's one of Frost's baby teeth," Oakastine explained.

"Who's Frost?"

"My dragon."

"Oh, that beauty! Thank you so much!" August exclaimed. She placed it back in the box. She adored it.

"I guess it's time for us to go." Carisie stood up and dusted off her skirt. She took August's hand and bowed at Oakastine. "I promise," she said.

Outside of Oakrale, August realized that they had left the stags back at the edge of the forest. She tugged at her mother's skirt and voiced her concern. "How will we get to Rafale and Gloria?" she asked.

"They will come, don't worry."

Carisie whistled. After a moment, they heard hoofbeats pounding, and the ground rumbled. As August watched their stags running towards them, something occurred to her.

"Mom, how did they reach us here?"

"Oh, there's a path."

"Then why on Earth did we ride that dragon?"

"Because Oakastine wanted us to have a grand arrival at Oakrale."

They both chuckled and welcomed their mounts. Carisie swung onto Gloria while August did her trademark belly-flop. In the orange sunset, they rode through the forest and the field of lavender, then through the aspen trees, and finally to Candrale.

It had been a long, exhausting day. August dismounted Rafale and handed him to the guard. A light bulb lit up in her head, and she decided to challenge her mother.

"The last one to reach the top of the stairs is the pig!" August exclaimed. She ran towards the door, and Carisie followed behind. August reached the winding staircase and began to climb it. Suddenly Carisie was getting ahead of her. August looked down and saw that Carisie was riding a cloud. "Hey! That's cheating!"

"You didn't say so before you started the game!" Carisie said, laughing.

August quickened her pace, taking two stairs at a time, and tried to catch her mother, but Carisie still got to the top first. August reached the top of the staircase, out of breath.

"You're the pig!" Carisie announced, chuckling.

August laughed too. "Oink, oink!"

MORE VEGETABLES

August finished her bath and then slipped back into her dress. She walked to the dinning room all by herself, without Traise to lead her there.

Carisie had told August to meet her here, but she was nowhere to be seen. She settled into a comfortable chair and waited, staring at the clock on the wall. *Tick-tock, tick-tock.* Minutes passed, and August began to worry. She stood up and began to pace the floor.

Finally the door opened and Carisie entered. "I'm sorry I'm late."

"It's OK. I guess I was just early," August said.

They sat down, and the chefs brought in the dinner dishes. August still hated vegetables, but it couldn't be as bad as what they had had for lunch. August took Carisie's hand and said a prayer. Then they began to eat. August gulped down the lettuce and broccoli. She chewed, swallowed, and drank from her glass. She tried to imagine that she was eating steak instead and ended up enjoying the food.

Dessert was crème brûlée. August couldn't believe her eyes; she loved crème brûlée. She dug her spoon in eagerly and scooped up a spoonful. She swallowed it immediately, scoop after scoop.

After dinner Carisie took August back to her bedroom. August changed and climbed into her soft bed. Carisie sat beside her on a stool. As August drifted into sleep, she thought she saw her mother's eyes fill with tears.

Follow the River

AUGUST WOKE UP and kicked her blankets away. She dragged herself out of bed and sat up, slumping groggily, and rubbed her eyes. She slipped into the new dress for today: it was white with a golden rose embroidered on the front and a long train in the back. A new pair of white flats had been placed by the window. August put them on.

Her mother entered the room with a white rose in her hand. With her delicate fingers, she tied a crown braid into August's golden hair and worked the white rose into it. "There, beautiful." August twirled around for her mother, and then they left the room together, holding hands.

Outside, August tried to mount Rafale correctly this time. She placed her hands on his back so her hands supported her weight, and then she jumped up and swang her right leg over. She sat upright and found herself mounted. She was happy with her accomplishment.

"That's good! You finally learned how to mount correctly," Carisie praised.

They trotted past the rows of aspen trees and turned right onto a sandy path. Dew-covered grass grew on either side. After a couple of minutes, they heard the sound of rushing water beating against rocks, and they slowed to a walk.

They came out onto a river. The path followed alongside it. August stared into the crystal-clear water to see white fish swimming and nibbling on water plants. A white jaguar leaf frog leaped across the river and landed on the other side. August enjoyed the sound of the rushing water. It reminded her of the river that flowed by her backyard at home on Earth.

"Always follow the river," Carisie said. "It leads you to the sea." They continued along the sandy path.

A Mysterious Tail

Eventually, they reached the point where the river and ocean met. The path grew sandier and wetter and then vanished into the sand. August realized she must be standing on the beach where her parents met. Waves rolled towards shore, seagulls flew above the sea, and baby turtles made their way to the water.

As they walked along the shore watching the waves devour the ground and then recede back into the ocean, August was stunned to notice a flapping tail in the water. It was long and colourful.

"Mom, I think I saw something big with a tail."

"Oh, you'll meet the mysterious tail soon," Carisie said.

Suddenly, a wave pushed a narwhal onto the shore. The narwhal's ivory tusk stretched nine feet long and glowed silver and gold. Sitting atop it was a human with a tail: a mermaid. She was a woman with long black hair that covered her chest, and the light-blue scales of her tail shone brightly under the sun.

August gazed at the mermaid's light-blue eyes, and then something hit her: it was the goddess of the water.

THE LEGEND OF THE MERMAID

M ERAIDA, GODDESS OF the water, guarded the ocean with her life. She had the upper torso of a human and the tail of a fish, and she lived underwater, the friend of sharks, killer whales, and other marine creatures. She was known as Mermaid Meraida, one of the three goddesses in Camberdice, and she was a fantastic hunter and incredible healer. She could heal people with her spells, and she was well known in the land of Camberdice.

THE GODDESS OF THE WATER

CARISIE GREETED THE mermaid, who smiled sweetly and waved at August. They dismounted, and Carisie introduced August.

"This is Meraida, goddess of the water. Meraida, this is my lost daughter."

"Carisa? Is that you?" The mermaid looked into August's eyes. "Yes, it is you. You're back!" "Sorry I can't hug you; I can't walk. I'll send you a kiss instead." She blew August a kiss.

August blushed and bowed to the Goddess. "Goddess Meraida, I prefer to be called August."

"Ah, *August*—a beautiful name for a strong girl. Would you like to explore the ocean?"

"I would, but I can't swim or breathe underwater."

"No worries!" Meraida raised her right hand and cast a spell over August and Carisie. "Now you can breathe underwater!"

She whistled towards the ocean and asked them to step closer to the water. August placed her feet into the water, and her mother did the same. A moment later, two shapes were swimming towards them. Two narwhals popped their heads out of the water. "Now, hop on, they'll bring you to Merale." August and Carisie laid flat on the creatures' backs and set off into the ocean.

MERMAIDS

Their narwhal mounts swam elegantly through the water, flipping their tails as they swam. August tried to hold her breath at first. She wasn't sure if she really could breathe underwater. But her mother was breathing normally and didn't seem to be having any problems at all. So August warily inhaled, then exhaled, then inhaled again just to make sure she was OK.

They were surrounded by marine creatures; they passed an orca, a shark, and a school of mermaids whose tails were red, blue, and green. Then they dove down deeper towards a tower that glowed brightly beneath them. The narwhals swam right up to the door. Meraida led them inside Merale.

The goddess of the water swam flexibly through the water, curving her body into an S-shape as she swam. Meanwhile, August found herself floating all over the place, constantly kicking the water to keep herself upright.

The interior of the palace was whitewashed, and seaweed climbed the walls. There was a treasure chest beside the throne.

"Say something," Meraida said to August.

"I'm breathing underwater!" August exclaimed in disbelied. "And I can talk!" Meraida laughed and turned to Carisie.

"Carisie, say something."

"I'm facing a woman with a tail," Carisie replied and chuckled.

Meraida led August to the treasure chest and pulled out a pearl necklace. "Whenever you wish to visit Merale again, put on these pearls, and you'll be able to breathe underwater." She handed the necklace to August and glanced briefly at Carisie. "Well, August, I wish you the best, if you know what I mean." She took August's hand and patted it softly.

"Yes, I know what you mean," August replied. She tried to smile.

"The breathing spell only lasts for half an hour, so I guess you two had better get back to the surface." Meraida whistled loudly. Two white dolphins swam up and scooped August and Carisie up with their snouts and onto their backs. Meraida waved goodbye to them. August held tightly on to the dolphin's dorsal fin as they were carried back to shore.

Dry Clothes

THE DOLPHINS DROPPED their passengers off at the shore, turned sideways in the water as if to wave goodbye with their pectoral fins, and vanished into the ocean. August felt her dress. It was dry. Her hair was dry too.

"How can we be dry when we just came out of the ocean?" she questioned her mother.

"I guess it was magic!" Carise replied. Gloria and Rafale cantered over to them. "Mount again, August, the correct way." August lifted herself off the ground, swung her right leg over, and sat up straight. "That's good!"

They followed the river home.

An Intense Morning Workout

The next morning, August slipped into her new dress and shoes and waited for her mother to pick her up. She yawned and stretched. Despite having just gotten up, she was still tired. Suddenly the door creaked open and her mother walked into the room.

"Oh, sorry, I should have knocked first," she apologized. She worked a simple braid into August's hair and tied the end with a horsehair. "Today will be a tiring day. Now that you've visited all the goddesses and explored this land, you're ready to start your training."

August could tell by the serious look on her loving mother's face that she had to take this training seriously. She had to do it not only for Camberice but also for Earth.

They rode their stags to the training field. The ground was covered in soft sand. There were jumps everywhere: red-and-yellow horizontal poles set up directly above each other. There was a target fixed to a tree. A steel bow and a quiver of arrows hung from a branch.

"Trot on," Carsie ordered. August kicked her stag forward. It broke into a fast trot at a smooth, easy pace. "Now change rein." August looked at Carisie, confused. "That means change direction. The field is a big rectangle. Let's say your left leg is the one closest to the outside edge of the field. To change rein, you'll turn to your right and go forward until you're close to the fence. Then you'll turn to your left so that your right leg is the outside leg and continue around the field."

August followed Carisie's instructions and and stirred Rafale to the right. Once she got closer to the fence, she turned him to the left.

"Good. Now we'll canter." Carisie picked up her rein and walked Gloria across the field. "To start a canter from a sitting trot, place your outside leg on the stag's belly and your inside leg closer to his flank. This time, don't kick, but squeeze with your heel." Carisie demonstrated and started to canter. Her hips rocked along with the stag's movement. "Shoulders back, sit up straight. Rock your hips along with the stag's movement."

August did as instructed, placing her outside leg on Rafale's belly and her inside leg closer to his flank. She squeezed with her heel, and Rafale broke into a slow canter.

"Now change rein," Carisie commanded.

August turned and changed direction. She tried to feel the stag's movements underneath her seat. She flopped around twice and then sat up straight with her shoulders back. When Rafale lifted off the ground, her hips rocked forward. She found her rhythym and moved along with him.

Carisie pointed to the first jump. Its pole was set the lowest of all the jumps. She cantered around the field and led Gloria up to the jump. As Gloria lifted her hooves, Carisie rose from her seat and leaned forwards, pressing her cheeks against Gloria's strong neck as they jumped. "Did you see what I did?" she asked August. She halted Gloria. "Now you try."

August gathered her courage and turned Rafale towards the jump. When he lifted his hooves and began to jump, August forgot to rise from her seat and lost her balance. She tumbled off Rafale and fell on the sandy ground.

"Loose stag!" Carisie shouted, and she stopped Rafale. "Again."

August mounted Rafale and tried the jump again. As soon as Rafale lifted his hooves, she leaned forward and pressed her cheek against Rafale's neck. After he landed, she sat up straight.

"Good! Now jump from the opposite direction."

August sighed and broke into a canter. She focused on the pole and charged Rafale forward. They were going too fast, and Rafale halted right before the jump. August was thrown into the air, and she landed harshly on the ground.

"Lesson two: never give up. Again!"

August got back on her trembling feet and mounted Rafale. She broke into a trot and gathered speed into a slower canter. She focused on the red and yellow and rose in her seat as soon as Rafale lifted his hooves. They sailed over the jump and landed safely on the other side.

"Good," Carisie pronounced. She pointed to a taller jump. "Now, this one."

August gulped. This pole was set at twice the height of the last one. She cantered and charged forward, pressing her cheek against Rafale's crest. She closed her eyes and enjoyed the feeling of flying. Rafale landed with a loud thump and slowed into a trot.

"Now, the opposite direction." August turned her stag and changed direction, she tackled the jump from the opposite direction, and they sailed over the pole gracefully, landing successfully on the other side. She slowed her stag into a trot and then a walk.

"That's enough for today," Carisie said. "You can explore Camberdice by yourself now. And remember to practice your cantering while you explore." Carisie led August out of the training field. "If you get lost, call me through the wind and I'll come to get you." She leaned over and kissed the top of August's head. "Goodbye for now."

THE FIRST THING THAT
CAME TO HER MIND

T HE FIRST THING that came to August's mind was visiting Matt. She liked him and wanted to go see him again. She took the path that led to Village Camberdice and cantered all the way there. Rafale plunged his hooves deep into the dirt and cantered with great speed across the land.

In the village, she walked Rafale on the asphalt road. She remembered in her heart the way to Matt's house. The villagers bowed at her and greeted her politely. She smiled awkardly and waved back; she wasn't used to this kind of treatment.

In front of Matt's house, Kristy was grooming her little pony. August dismounted and walked over. The little girl stopped what she was doing and ran over to unbolt the gate and welcome August in.

"Kristy, is your brother here?"

"Yeah, he's in the backyard grooming his new stallion." She pointed the way and smiled broadly.

"Thanks!" August went to the backyard. Matt was grooming his horse with great care, not missing a spot. "Hey," she said softly.

"Hey, it's great to see you here! What are you up to?" he replied, grinning.

"My mom allowed me to explore on my own, so I decided to visit you."

"I see. Do you want to go for a ride? I want to try out my new stallion."

"Sure." August felt very comfortable with Matt. She was probably falling for him. "My stag's out front. I'll meet you there." She skipped back to Rafale and mounted him. "Oh, Rafale, please make me look good," she whispered into the stag's ears.

Matt came out to meet her. He looked very fine on his new stallion. "Where do you want to go?" he asked, his eyes gleaming.

"Anywhere."

"Let's go to the beach, then."

They headed for the river that flowed into the sea.

WHAT WOULD YOU WISH FOR?

ONCE THEY REACHED the beach, they dismounted and walked on foot together. August looked at the ocean and imagined Meraida swimming gracefully with her fellow marine creatures. Matt led her to a huge rock and they sat down on it.

"So, are you scared about having to face the Son of Earth?"

"Yes, I am. But I can't show it. The fate of two lands, Camberdice and Earth, is in my hands. I can't let you guys down."

"You wont. I have faith in you," Matt said. "If you could have anything, what would you wish for?"

"To win the battle without any lives being lost."

"You can do it, I know." He hugged August and she could feel her face getting red. "I'll be praying for you. Kristy will too."

Now I really am falling for him, August thought. She looked up at the sky. "The sky is so beautiful today. But someday it might all be darkness." She suddenly felt very afraid that she might fail.

"No, it wont." Matt looked into her eyes. "You will succeed, I'm certain. Everybody has faith in you, August. Your return gave us hope."

They sat on the rock for the rest of the evening, talking about Camberdice's future and watching the sun set and vanish into the deep ocean.

"I should get back before dark, or my mom is going to kill me," August announced. She stood up and prepared to leave.

"Let me send you home," Matt offered.

They got on their mounts and headed off to Candrale. August was certain that Matt liked her.

Goodbye, Romeo

At Candrale, August saw her mother standing out front, waiting for her to return.

Carisie greeted Matt, smiling. "So Romeo finally brought my daughter home," she joked. "Did you two have fun today?" August blushed and walked Rafale forward.

She waved as Matt disappeared in the distance. Carisie helped her to dismount.

August had a quick bath before meeting her mother in the dining room. While they waited for dinner to be served, Carisie placed her hands on the table and smiled sweetly.

"You like Matt, don't you?" she asked, smiling broadly.

"No! Why would I?" August blurted out.

"Oh, dear. I can tell that he likes you too."

"Maybe, but I only like him as a friend," August insisted.

The chefs walked into the room with the dinner dishes. August readied herself and lifted the cover off her plate: broccoli, lettuce, and carrots. She sighed and started to eat.

Dessert was cheesecake. Carisie chuckled to see August gulping it down. She loved it.

After dinner, August went to bed and slept soundly. She would be ready for tomorrow's training.

Arrows and Blisters

"We won't need our stags today," Carisie said when they reached the training ground next morning. "You'll be learning how to hunt."

They dismounted and entered the field. Carisie removed the bow and arrows from the tree with the target. "This used to be my bow. Now it is yours. Today, you'll be a hunter."

Carisie pulled out an arrow and demonstrated what to do before handing the bow and arrow over to August. August placed the arrow on the arrow rest. "Look at the tip of the arrow and aim for your target," Carisie said. August nodded. "Then draw the string back. Your hand should be at the nocking point."

August posititoned herself and aimed for her target. She leveled her eyes with the arrow's tip and drew the wire string back. Then she released it. The arrow flew straight and hit the red centre circle of the target. Its sharp point stuck deep into the tree trunk.

"Dead shot, clean kill," Carisie said from behind August. She walked up to the tree, pulled out the arrow, and handed it to August. "Nice shot," she praised. "Now step farther back."

August backed up a few steps and repositioned herself. She drew the string back, leveled her eyes with the tip of the arrow, and released the wire string. The arrow blasted straight ahead and hit the target with a thud.

"Good job!" Carisie said. "You're a natural hunter and warrior."

"Your turn!" August said brightly, handing the bow to Carisie. She was desperate to watch her mother shoot.

Carisie took the bow and slotted the arrow onto the arrow rest. She took a step back and observed the target. Without any hestition, she drew the string back and released. The arrow traveled rapidly and plunged deep into the tree trunk. August went forward to examine the target. The arrow was a perfect bull's-eye.

"How on Earth did you do that?" August asked, shocked.

"I'm an archer. I've been practicing for years," Carisie said modestly. She swung the bow over her shoulder and walked towards August. "One day, you'll be as good as I am."

August looked at her own fingers. They were blistered and bruised. "No way, I'll never be as good as you are." She pulled the arrow out of the tree. "Do you think I'm ready?" she asked quietly.

Carisie rubbed August's cheek and tucked a loose hair behind her ear. "You have only a couple more things to learn: how to cast glow and how travel through the portal without going through the Breakdown."

"And then I'll be ready to face the Son of Earth?"

"Yes, you will. But don't worry, I will be watching you from the clouds. I promise that you survive the battle."

Back in August's room that night, Carisie opened the box that held Paul's old leartherbound book. "Bring this along tomorrow. Together, we will learn how to cast glow." She handed the book to August and left the room.

THE GLOW

AUGUST CRAWLED OUT of her bed the next morning and started her routine all over again. Before she headed out the door, she grabbed the box in her blistered hands, and then she rushed for the stairs. She sat on the railing and glided down the staircase—something she had loved doing back on Earth—landed on her feet, and walked out of the front door.

Carisie was waiting patiently for August. Together, they walked to the training field. August glanced at the amethyst ring on her mother's ring finger, The stone shone brightly in the sunlight.

"Is that a wedding ring?" she asked curiously.

Carisie inhaled deeply. "Yes, it is. From your father."

"Oh. I'm sorry for asking."

Her mother shook her head as if it did not matter.

At the field, Carisie opened the box and removed the book. She read the first page thoroughly, trying to absorb as much information as possible.

The Spell to Cast Glow

With your hands together, imagine the glow that shines from the sun. Feel the warmth slowly emanating from your hands.

Recite "Shine to the sun" under your breath, and then open your hands to send the glow.

To my dearest daughter, Carisa, from your father, Paul.

"He wrote this for me?" August asked, reading the last sentence over and over again.

"Yes, you're the only one who can cast glow. He knew that one day you would return to finish what must be finished."

They prepared to try casting the spell. Carisie read the spell aloud. "'With your hands together, imagine the glow that shines from the sun. Feel the warmth slowly emanating from your hands.'"

August tried to imagine the glow around the sun. She pictured hot flames and blinding light beaming from the sun. Suddenly, she felt as though her hands were burning. "That hurts!" she shrieked. She opened her eyes in shock and stared at her own hands. The burning sensation melted away.

Carisie looked into August's terrified face in alarm. "What hurts?"

"Something was burning my hands."

"The spell must have been working. Let's try it again."

August closed her eyes and clasped her hands together. She pictured the sun's glow again until her hands were warm and she felt them glowing. "Shine to the sun," she muttered.

"Now open your hands," her mother said. August pulled her hands apart, sending a beam of light into the sky. "It works! But your light is still too faint. Never mind, this light should still be enough to delay the strike of the eclipse and give us more time to plan our strategy."

Carisie asked August to cast the light again. August did so. She sent another beam of light up around the sun. She was feeling really excited. This was her first time using magic. "Was my father's glow a lot stronger than mine?" she asked.

"Yes, it was. Your father's glow was bright enough to cover not only the sun but the entire land. But for now, yours will do just fine," Carisie said affectionately.

"So when will I cast the glow?"

"I'll tell you when it's necessary." Carisie placed the book back in the box. "But now let's move on to travelling through portals. I'll teach you how to travel without experiencing the Breakdown."

"Travel to where?"

"Between Earth and Camberdice."

On hearing Carisie's answer, August was both shocked and happy. She couldn't wait to return to Earth. She had had some amazing experiences in Camberdice: using magic, riding a pegasus and a unicorn, standing on a cloud. But still, she was badly missing her Earth parents and her pets. She missed minute-cooked steak and to-die-for pizza. She even missed the mean girls at school a little bit.

THE PORTAL TO EARTH

CARISIE TOOK AUGUST'S hand and recited a spell. "For the equines travel through with hope." A portal appeared before them, glimmering in shades of violet and bright blue.

"Why is it purple?" August asked.

"Because I'm holding your hand."

They stepped into the portal, still holding hands. Inside the portal, it was dark and August felt numb. A moment later, they were in an entirely different place. August felt no pain, no Breakdown, unlike the first time she'd gone through the portal. Her mind raced. *Is this Earth? Where are we? Where are Mom and Dad? Can I have a slice of pizza before we go?*

"This is Earth, August," Carisie said quietly. "Now, you must do Earth a favour and cast your glow."

August pushed away the thought of food and concentrated. She put her hands together and felt them grow warm. Then she recited the spell and opened her hands. A bright light blasted into the sky and surrounded the sun.

"I can't believe I'm using magic," August said. She pinched herself to make sure she wasn't dreaming and turned towards her mother.

"Are you ready to go? You can open the portal this time."

"What am I supposed to say again?"

"'For the equines travel through with hope,'" Carisie replied, taking August's hand. "If you are holding on to someone or riding something, they'll travel along with you."

August nodded. She waved her hand and recited the spell. A bright purple and blue portal apppeared before them. Mother and daughter entered the portal and everything went dark, cold, and numb again.

THE DARKNESS RETURNS

CARISIE COULD TELL something was wrong. She could feel something evil slipping into her land. She rushed outside and observed the sky. It was still bright. She closed her eyes and tried to sense what was happening. The darkness was coming. Shocked, Carisie's eyes flew open. She ran back inside and up to August's room.

August was still asleep. Carisie had no choice but to wake her. "August, you have to get up now!" August rubbed her eyes. "The darkness is slipping in!" Carisie continued. August turned to look out the window. Everything seemed perfectly fine. The sun was shining and the sky was bright blue.

"Mom, it's clear outside. There's no darkness."

"No, I can feel it! It's slipping in," Carisie argued.

"I'll cast glow now." August propped herself up and got out of bed.

"No!" Carisie held on to August's hand tightly. "It's too dangerous. We don't know exactly when the eclipse will strike, but it's coming soon. I can feel it."

"But that makes no sense. I just cast glow yesterday."

"I think the darkness is too evil. We need to inform the other two goddesses. They probably sense it as well. The land feels different."

It was the first time August had seen her mother lose her cool, the first time her mother had looked afraid. Things must indeed be serious.

In her own room, Carisie took out a piece of paper and a quill.

Dear Okastine,

The purpose of this dove letter is to inform you that darkness is starting to slip into our land. I can feel it. Perhaps you already have. Please pass this message on to Meraida. I'll plan a stratergy with August.

For the safety of our land,
Carisie

Carisie rolled the paper quickly and secured it with a golden ribbon. She and August ran to the paddock and rang the bell. After a nerve-wracking five minutes, August finally saw a bird flying towards them. Carisie whispered to it, and they watched the bird fly away with the letter before they rushed back to the palace.

Carisie ordered all the guards and maids to return home and lock their doors. Then they went into Carisie's room and closed the doors and windows and drew the curtains.

Carisie sat down and rubbed her temples. Her face was pale and her eyes were dark and full of tears. She was trembling.

"He's here," she said. She took August's face in her hands and August's heart thumped in her chest. Carisie closed her eyes. "He is here, and he will start with Earth."

THE HUNT

August mounted Rafale and galloped off. *Bring him into Camberdice. We'll finish our business here,* she thought.

She recalled what Carisie had told her. "During the eclipse, he can travel between the lands freely, without even a portal."

August was terrified. Dark clouds covered what had just been a blue sky. Shadow covered the sun. The land was nothing but darkness. If she could have burst into tears, she would have. She urged Rafale to pick up his speed. As they rode, she raised her hand and recited the spell to create a purple portal before them. She kicked Rafale forward and through the portal.

Everything went dark and cold, and then August's senses returned and they were in a different place. A clash of thunder growled fiercely and lightning hit the ground nearby. The sky was pitch black. Her surroundings looked extremely familiar. She was *home.*

Rafale reared on his hind legs. His eyes were white. "Calm down. Easy, boy," August whispered. She had to find the Son of

Earth before anybody was killed. As they galloped through the darkness, Rafale breathed heavily, letting out puffs of smoke. Again the thunder growled and a flash of lightning struck a tree right in front of them. The tree began to fall. It was too late to slow Rafale down, so August charged him forward and they jumped through the tree branches to safety.

But Rafale halted. Before them stood a dark, tall figure with white skin and eyes as grey as clouds. His shoulders were covered in black feathers. He cracked his neck to the side and flexed a claw-like hand. "Ah, Carisa, the goddess's daughter. I'll tell your father that you're on your way to meet him in hell."

August immediately kicked Rafale into a gallop. She sensed his chest widen and compress until they breathed as one, galloping as fast as lightning across the dark land. August cast the spell to open a portal, and Rafale leaped into it. They fell into deep darkness.

FACING DEATH

Back in Camberdice, August raced into the woods, the only place she could hide. Her muscles tensed, her heart beat wildly in her chest, and her mind raced. Rafale stretched out his neck and extended his legs as he galloped to cover as much ground as possible. August looked up. The sun was completely gone, covered by an opaque shadow. A cloud of bats flew by. What had once been a majestic land was now only darkness.

From behind them August heard a *whiz*; there was an arrow coming straight for her! She leaned to her right and the arrow missed her right ear by about an inch. She could feel Rafale gather speed, trying to escape the deadly Son of Earth.

Then August noticed Frost the dragon circling the sky. She spread her wings and dove, spitting out hot flames. The Son of Earth swung his bow forward, took aim at the flying creature, and shot. The arrow punched through the white dragon's throat. Blood spilled in the sky. Frost groaned in pain and fell to the ground. She struggled to get up.

August gasped and tears filled her eyes. Anger sparked in her heart. The Son of Earth was a cruel devil. August felt pure hatred for him.

She dismounted Rafale, fixed her eyes onto his, and calmed him down. "Go get help. Find Oakastine," she whispered. She watched the stag disappear into the thick woods. Then she hid herself behind a huge tree trunk. Her heart kicked in her chest as the death of Frost the dragon replayed in her mind. She clenched her fists and told herself to calm down. She had to be brave for both her lands.

Thunder rolled loudly above the clouds. August took deep breaths to try to stop trembling. She couldn't feel her legs. She closed her eyes and listened to her surroundings. The seconds felt like hours. She didn't know when the devil would find her; she could only wait and pray for help to come. Then she remembered that her mother was watching her from the clouds. She raised her head and prayed, her stomach fluttering. A crash of lightning hit a nearby tree, breaking it in half. August jumped and her heart pounded. She now knew the real meaning of the word *fear*. It definitely wasn't something you felt being chased by a dog or being punished by a teacher; it was facing death and trying to survive.

THE HERO STAG

AUGUST HEARD FOOTSTEPS approaching. Her heart stopped for a moment and then raced faster. She heard the Son of Earth laugh wickedly.

"I can sense your fear from here, Carisa. Come out now, you little brat." His voice was sharp and clear and piercing. "Come out before I destroy you." He laughed again.

Is he right in the head? August wondered. She stayed on her feet, ready to fight, counted to three, and then stepped out from behind the trunk.

"You want me, don't you? So you can control both lands?" She paused to give him a chance to answer, but nothing came out of the devil's mouth. "Well, no offense, but what makes you think you deserve to?"

The devil cracked his neck to his right. "You're asking for death!" he roared angrily. He swung his bow forward and aimed at August. From out of nowhere, Rafale raced towards her and leaped forward just as the devil released his arrow. *Thwack!* The arrow struck her brave white stag in the neck. August's heart dropped.

Rafale collapsed to the ground and tossed his head and kicked. His antlers dulled and darkened. His eyes lost their spirit. Then he lay motionless, bleeding heavily from the throat. Blood spread over the ground in all directions. August cried over the lifeless stag who had saved her life.

That was when she found her strength, the strength to battle with the darkness. The flame that had sparked in her soul grew bigger until it was hot enough to push her into action.

YOU MESSED WITH THE
WRONG GIRL

She stood up, furious. "Why would you do that?" August shouted in the devil's face.

"Don't question your lord," he said, grinning evilly. He aimed his arrow at August's throat. "Say goodbye to your mom now."

"Look into my eyes!" August screamed. "I see your weakness, your fear, and your insecurity."

The devil lowered his bow for a moment with a trace of uncertainty. "Don't try to fool me!" he said, and he aimed again.

"I am not! Your weakness is your heart!"

The devil stumbled, obviously shocked to hear what August said, and the arrow was released harmlessly into the air. It landed beside August. Her heart jumped. *It's now or never.* She pulled the arrow out of the ground and charged towards the devil, running as fast as she could.

"Lesson number one: face your fear!" With all her strength, August plunged the arrow deep into the Son of Earth's heart. She looked deep into his eyes with fury. His face paled and his pupils shrank. He wrapped his claw-hand around the arrow's shaft and tried to pull it out of his wound. "Lesson number two: never give up!" Still flaming with anger, August pushed the arrow deeper into the devil's chest, causing him to roar in pain. "And this," she shouted, "is killing the animals!" The wound widened and a swarm of bats flooded out of it and raced into the sky. "You messed with the wrong girl," August growled. The Son of Earth shattered into a hundred pieces and then vanished.

THE SUN RETURNS

AUGUST STUMBLED BACK and collapsed onto the ground. She crawled back towards Rafale and stroked his cheek and then pulled the arrow out of his throat. Above, the dark shadow had faded away and the sun had returned, brighter than ever. August thanked the stag for saving her life and kissed his forehead. "Thank you," she whispered, hoping he would hear her from heaven.

Carisie appeared before August and hugged her tightly in her arms. Then Oakastine arrived and bowed to her. Everyone was crying. Raindrops fell from the bright sky, washing away the spilled blood. Meraida had called for rain.

Meraida sounded the horn to inform the villagers that the darkness had been defeated. They cheered and crowded around Candrale, waiting for August's return. In his home, Matt smiled in relief, holding his sister in his arms. *I knew you could do it,* he thought.

AUGUST RETURNS HOME

AFTER THE DEFEAT of the Son of Earth had been celebrated, Carisie allowed August to go back to Earth. Carisie, Oakastine, Matt, and Kirsty all stood in a line on Hill Camberdice, preparing to send August home. The pegasus Storm dove from the sky and landed on the hill to bid August goodbye too. August patted his nose and combed through his mane. Oakastine made sure that August had Frost's baby tooth and thanked her for everything she'd done. Matt stood by quietly with his sister. And Carisie hugged August tightly in her arms, trying to hide her tears.

August recited the spell that opened the portal. She stepped forward.

"Wait!" Matt shouted. He ran to August and kissed her on the cheek. "Now you can go."

August blushed. "I'll miss you and Kristy, and her Shetland pony."

"You can visit Camberdice whenever you want," Carisie said, giving her another tight hug.

"Then I guess I'll see you guys soon," August said. She waved goodbye and walked into the purple light. The portal closed behind her.

ABOUT THE AUTHOR

READING PLAYS A big role in my life; writing too. I hope this story inspires your imagination and the little creative voice in your mind. I started writing when I was around eleven but I never finished any of my stories, due to either laziness or a lack of confidence.

Then one day, an extraordinary story came into my mind. I tried really hard to finish this one, sitting at my desk from 11 a.m. to 12 a.m. for countless days. And that's how *Two Lands* came to be. It was inspired by the tiniest things in life. A little thing can always lead to something greater than you expect. One little thing is your imagination.

Instead of spending your holiday sleeping and playing video games, why not write a story that reflects your personality and your interests? All you need is a pen and a notebook. Anything is possible when you write from the heart. Writing isn't easy—sometimes when you run out of ideas, it can be frustrating—but that's what makes it interesting.

Happy writing!

Lee Shirley